Beneath A Barren Sky

Carolyn Purcell Jaco

Sissortail Press

Beneath a Barren Sky

© 2023 Carolyn Purcell Jaco

ISBN: 979-8-9878743-0-1

First Edition, Published in the United States

This is a work of fiction inspired by true stories and real events drawn from a variety of sources. Names, characters, events, and incidents are the products of the author's imagination or used in a fictitious manner. Any resemblance to actual persons, living or dead, is purely coincidental. The opinions expressed are those of the characters and should not be confused with the author's.

Scissortail Press, 876 Hartshorne Lake Road, Hartshorne, Oklahoma 74547

Contents

Dedicated to
Nancy Ann Lusk Purcell
1928 – 2002

Reviews of Beneath a Barren Sky:
"...wholesome escapism and a bit of nostalgia." – Reedsy
"...a fresh new voice." – V. Sims
"...evocative and poignant...heartwarming and inspiring."
-Online Book Club

Brady Street

JANUARY IN DAVENPORT, IOWA, can be brutal. When Ginger Lusk felt her first contraction, she tried to call her husband, Parke, but the lines were down. In 1928, blizzards brought traffic to a standstill. Road clearing equipment was almost nonexistent. So, Ginger tried to prepare herself to deliver this baby into the world without the safety and comfort of a hospital. She bathed, scrubbed the floor in front of the fireplace, and gathered towels and blankets, just in case. By the time Parke came home from the office, her water had broken and her pains were five minutes apart.

Parke had put chains on the car tires to get home and hoped he could make it to the hospital. Two blocks before they reached the entrance, the Model A Ford became hopelessly stuck in a snowdrift and he had to mostly carry his wife the rest of the way. She delivered one half hour later just as Parke fainted against the light switch. Chaos ensued, during which a nurse accidentally groped the doctor, instruments crashed to the floor, an ether bottle was broken, and the anesthesiologist fell over the prone father while reaching for the light switch. Exhaustion, as well as shock at witnessing the gore of childbirth, may well have been the reason for his fainting. After this amazing incident, St. Luke's Hospital banned fathers from the delivery room for the next thirty-seven years.

It was their firstborn and Ginger had wanted everything to be dreamily perfect. She had made herself pale pink, blue, and beige gowns and bed jackets, with hair ribbons to match, to wear during the traditional ten-day stay in the hospital.

Those first few years of their marriage were like an idyllic dream; their days were filled with sweet naiveté, optimism, and blissful happiness. There was a small painting hanging on the living room wall, a sort of castle in billowing rosy clouds against a blue-black sky. The oak-framed watercolor was a wedding present from an *avant-garde* artist friend. It was clearly a phallic symbol. Ginger said it depicted love. Maybe, in the beginning of love and marriage, sex is all that really matters, but then it slips into the background as more formidable aspects take over the business of life.

During the period before the Great Depression, the H.C. Lusk & Sons food brokerage business in Davenport flourished. Parke's father, "Handsome Harry," as he was known when he was younger, made deals with the potato farmers in Iowa, Wisconsin, and Illinois to buy their entire crops. In turn, he sold the potatoes to the grocers for an outrageous profit. The enterprise was successful and he became known in the Midwest trade as the "Potato King."

Harry's introversion began in 1929 when the stock market crashed and he lost his money and his confidence. He was no longer the self-important man of the photograph of the H.C. Lusk & Sons staff taken years earlier. The old black and white print showed Harry at the center of fifteen assorted relatives, including distant cousins, posing jauntily in their shirtsleeves and suspenders. The gold chain across his paunch depicted the spirit of a profitable era.

The young Harry had been brought up in Albany, Illinois, where his grandfather had settled because it was rumored that a large railroad center was slated to emerge there. Harry was born in 1858, one of eight children. His father, Charles, was a successful dry goods merchant who built a handsome big frame house for the family with an adjacent brick building. He also founded a bank in the town and though the railroad never materialized, the town flourished well enough as a Mississippi river boat landing and small provincial village.

In 1866, a fire broke out in Charles' storage building down by the dock. A horseback rider, passing through town on his way West to dig for gold, spotted the smoke. By the time he arrived at the scene, flames were reaching for help. The rider whirled about looking for anyone to report the burning sight when someone yelled to him, "Get Lusk, his place—FIRE!" as he pointed up the hill to the house. The adventurer dug in his heels, racing toward the Lusk home. He was nearly to the front door when someone flung it open. The horse was flying with such momentum that he charged right through the entrance, clattering up the stairs to the second floor and back again, before finally halting with a screech in the front hall.

The storage building fire was too hot for a bucket brigade to make any difference regardless of it being at the dock. Fortunately, Charles had the resources to rebuild. It was, after all, only storage, not their beautiful home. Harry witnessed this through the eyes of an eight-year-old and he kept it with him. By the time he was married and settled in Davenport, the tale was told with ever-increasing drama to his three children to ensure its place in family lore.

P ARKE WAS AN OLD family name going back to Martha Washington's side of the family. They said she was his great, great, great aunt. George was Martha's second husband, so he was not exactly kin. Nonetheless, Parke believed he was of aristocratic breeding and, despite his sweet nature, could be a bit of a snob. Parke had the slim, tall, graceful physique that suited him for sports such as tennis, golf, and horsemanship. His gray-green eyes had the Irish droopy canthus lids, which gave him a sympathetic expression. His sable-colored hair tended to curl, but he slicked it straight back with water, parting it in the middle, which was the fashion of the day.

At twelve years old, he began taking riding and golfing lessons at the country club, where he made many friends. The club was like a second home to the family who all spent much time there. Parke loved the horses and enjoyed getting to know their personality quirks. He rode them both in the ring and on the trails on a rotating basis to make sure they would remember him. He spent time with the groomsmen learning skills of animal husbandry and, sometimes, would simply hang out with the horses while he read a book.

In 1892, a Chicago industrialist built the Davenport residence now owned by the H.C. Lusk family. It had a black marble fireplace mantle and an eight-foot-tall beveled glass front door. Hand carved banisters on the sweeping front stairway led up to four bedrooms. The attic was for servant quarters. Harry bought the property in 1902 when Parke was seven years old. The house defined their family and shaped their opinion of themselves. Harry's wife, Miranda, or Mimi for short, was the most gracious host, throwing elaborate parties. Parke's mother also liked to shock people with her disregard for protocol by doing things like kicking off her buttonhook, high-heeled shoes and sitting on the couch with her feet curled up under her skirts no matter who was visiting.

Parke's best friend was Billy Velie, the son of a prominent manufacturing family, who, among other things, had built the Velie automobile. The two boys would often roam the rambling hills of the Velie estate, located only a few miles north and across the river in Moline, half-heartedly hunting but mostly exploring. One day, when they were fifteen, as they shuffled single-file through a golden Indian summer woods with their guns carelessly slung over their shoulders, Parke, in the lead, tripped over a log, causing his gun to fire. The bullet shot through Billy's heart. He died there, on a bed of colorful maple leaves with a ray of sunshine sifting through the branches to warm him against the autumn chill.

Despite this devastating event, Parke's winning personality propelled him as he grew into a man. Parke never doubted he was the most charismatic person at any gathering. Everyone looked his way when he entered a room, laughing, confident, in his linen suit, which hung loosely on his lanky frame. He loved to be the center of attention, the life of the party. He sang bawdy little ditties at the piano or recited bits of poetry.

> *I want free life and I want fresh air; and I sigh*
> *for the canter after the cattle, the cracks of the*
> *whips like shots in a battle.*

If he could bring tears to your eyes, he was delighted.

> *Lasca was dead! I gouged out a grave a few feet*
> *deep, and there in earth's arms I laid her to*
> *sleep; and the little gray hawk hangs aloft in*
> *the sky. And the black snake glides and glitters*
> *and slides into a rift in a cottonwood tree; and*
> *the buzzard sails on, and comes and is gone.*

He carefully calculated his intonations to evoke emotion.

When he was seventeen, he had a brilliant revelation, which made him want to be on stage forever. An audition for a part in the senior class play called for him to do a monologue and he was the first on stage. As he walked across to a chair set at the center, a spotlight came upon him so he could not see the audience. There he was, alone in a circle of light, becoming his character.

"My God!" he exclaimed later to a confidant. "It was as if that circle of light held me safely in its arms. I could be anybody. The audience was mine."

Ever since then, any success in business or love felt diminished in comparison. There was a missing element; that need for inner fulfillment through adventure or creativity was always elusive and just beyond his grasp.

After high school, Harry sent Parke first to Cornell, where he studied pre-law, and then on to law school at Yale. His grades were far from perfect and Harry admonished him often for not taking life seriously. He greatly enjoyed beating his classmates at chess and golf, and flirting with girls in town. He graduated at the end of winter term 1918, and left for boot camp as the country joined the European allies. Because of his education and relative maturity compared to the eighteen-year-old recruits, the Army assigned him as Captain in a cavalry unit. He was stationed in France where his expert handling of horses won him the care of an enormous Friesian war horse, an unusual find in that place. In another time, this magnificent beast would have remained whole to propagate the breed, but instead it had recently been castrated for use in the war effort. Those less suitable became sustenance for the troops. Parke bonded quickly with the horse and, though troops were discouraged from naming their steeds, Parke called his mount Ares, after the Greek god of war.

While on mission with a British squadron, a bullet hit Ares in an ambush. As the rest of the men rode after the assailants, Ares slowed and sunk to his knees. Parke was unable to extract his foot from the stirrup before Ares rolled on his side, breaking and pinning Parke's leg. Unable to reach his rifle, which was also under the horse, there was no way to release Ares from his pain. Parke lay there for thirty minutes, speaking softly into Ares' ear of bravery, strength, service, and honor. He told Ares that he would be free soon to soar with the gods on golden wings. When the men returned to rescue Parke and get him to safety, they shot the animal while Parke tried to hide his tears.

Leaving tht amazing animal in that terrible war-torn place had a profound effect on him. At first glance, onlookers might think that Parke had the bird of Paradise by the tail, but deep down he was a discontented man. Ghosts from the past haunted him.

> *Last night... Ah, yesternight, betwixt her lips*
> *and mine, there fell thy shadow. Cynarae.*

He muttered Dowson's curious poem in his cups. Cynarae meant an ideal, a dream of perfection, always floating beyond the reaching fingertips. Parke yearned for recognition as a performer. Unwittingly, his own family had instilled this in him when he was a child. At family gatherings, everyone was encouraged to recite a poem, enact a story, play the piano, or sing. Ever since that moment in the spotlight, Parke longed for more meaning, understanding, and perhaps glorification, too. It was difficult to be complacent having known he could do more. Meanwhile, it was the pressures from his mother and father to conform to the banalities of their world, including the expectation to marry and settle down, that plagued him most.

When the war was over, Parke and three other wild young rakes piled into a topless touring car and took off for California, a trip highly punctuated with flat tires and stuck-in-the-mud stories. He worked in Hollywood briefly finding odd jobs, sometimes on movie sets as a background player where he met and mingled with some of the stars of the early 1920s.Whenever horses were in a scene, Parke gravitated there to lend a hand. His earnings were meager and his living quarters were embarrassing. His parents were not impressed and felt he was chasing an impractical acting dream. They needed his help in the family business and thought it was time for him to settle down. In 1923, he traveled by train back to his family in Davenport.

His sister Dorothy, who was nicknamed Dottie, was two years younger than Parke and had been married with children for seven years. Parke's younger brother, Allen, had been too young to serve in the war. When Allen graduated from high school, Harry sent him to the Wharton School of the University of Pennsylvania to study business and economics. Allen was shorter than Parke and dark haired. He carried a more serious and somber disposition than his brother and Harry hoped he would become a great asset to the company. After four years at Wharton studying with the best and brightest professors, Allen became the financial manager of the family business at twenty-three years old. He was a steady talent in the office, helping to expand their product line into many different types of dry goods. Parke, with his good looks and charming personality, was well suited for sales. The company bought him a car and challenged him to expand their reach. For three years, he drove in ever-expanding circles on horrible roads to sell their wares to retailers in Iowa, Illinois, and Missouri.

Now at the age of thirty-one, this charming lover-man was struggling to keep body and soul together, occasionally slipping into a bottle to hide from the world. His sensitivity and creative nature kept him on the edge of being satisfied with his lot. His affluent parents paved the way for him to rejoin the country club under his own name when he returned to Davenport. That is where eligible girls sought him out for dinner dates and long horseback rides on the miles of trails beyond the stables. Sadly, he never could find the one who would hold his interest for any length of time.

Until he met Ginger. Five-foot-two, eyes-of-blue, Ginger, with chestnut-brown hair, Betty Grable legs, and a contagious laugh. The first time he saw her she was dancing to a dizzying, tinny recording of the old jazz standard, "Tiger Rag" atop a table, raising hell at a party. Ginger Morgan was a first-year student at Augustana College across the River in Rock Island, engaged to a young doctor, and she was about to lose her footing as the table toppled. Parke caught her as she fell, saving her from what might have been numerous contusions. It was love at first flight.

Well, that was the story Parke told while holding court at parties, much to the delight of his audiences. Real life is never quite that simple. Parke had a habit of testing his acting skills to see if he was convincing before telling the truth. This fanciful boy-meets-girl story was a complete fabrication told sheerly for entertainment purposes.

P ARKE'S FARTHEST ACCOUNT ON his sales routes was in the tiny town of Hardenville, Missouri, on the Arkansas border. Richard Morgan and his wife, Myrtle, who everyone called Baba—a childhood nickname that endured time—owned the general store there. Parke found them entirely by accident when he lost his way on the backroads and heavy rain was starting to make passage through the mud impossible. Parke ducked into their store and Richard greeted him warmly. He advised that Parke should stay the night with them in the spare room at their house across the street. The Morgan's were having problems with their supply chain and were eager to discuss an account with Lusk & Sons brokerage over dinner. While Parke cleaned himself up for dinner, he could smell the most delicious aromas of savory spiced roasting meat and potatoes coming from the kitchen. When he entered their dining room to take his place at the table, he discovered the Morgan's seventeen-year-old daughter, Ginger. She was breathtaking in a simple, southern, country sort of way.

He managed to visit the Morgan's once a month for six months, while many of his other clients only saw him quarterly. Parke told hilarious stories in front of the fire and Ginger and her parents always looked forward to his visits. When it was time to say goodbye, Ginger often feigned a continuing conversation as an excuse to walk him to his car, where she flirtatiously stood on the side rail to prevent him from getting into the driver's seat. Afraid he might scare her off and ruin his chances, he waited until several visits before asking for a parting kiss. She blushed a deep scarlet and stared at the ground, gathering her nerve. She had become quite smitten with him and wanted this first kiss to be special and perfect. Finally, she lifted her chin just enough to see him through her eyelashes. He gently took her chin in his fingers and lifted her lips to his. They both knew it was true love.

On his next visit, as they sat around the dinner table, Baba told Parke that Ginger had cooked the meal, a sumptuous roast pork, watercress salad, and sweet potatoes. Ginger piped up and said, "Not only can I cook but I can sew, drive a car, and dance the Charleston." She flashed Parke an enormous smile.

Baba said, "Now Gin, don't go braggin' about yourself."

"I don't mind," said Parke. "Learning about all the talents of Ginger is my pleasure." He matched her smile while they locked eyes for several moments.

Back at home, Parke spoke to his parents about his courtship of Ginger. His father was reticent. "Tell us about her, again, Parke," Harry demanded. "Is she educated? Is she going to be able to navigate the social circles of the country club?"

"Oh, stop!" said his mother. "If you love each other that is all that matters."

After a brief courtship, Parke asked Richard for his daughter's hand and their blessing. That night, the two of them sat before the fire while Ginger dramatically tossed, one after another, all her love letters from past suitors into the flames. They then settled down to discuss the logistics of a wedding. Parke's parents were Christian Scientists and would not be offended by a secular marriage. Parke himself was a confirmed agnostic and only wanted to make sure the Morgan's Baptist beliefs were properly honored. The Morgan's thought a marriage illegitimate without the blessing of a minister. They also could not afford to leave their store to come to Davenport for a wedding. Ginger just wanted to get married to the love of her life as quickly as possible.

The next afternoon, the local Baptist minister joined them in marriage in the Morgan's living room. The bride wore a green crepe dress with a hole in the sleeve. The wedding band was a narrow silver token purchased in the next town over. Parke drove off with his bride after Ginger's tearful goodbye to her parents. They took two days to get home to Davenport, stopping for ice cream, a view of a lake, or a chance to just sit together and talk about the future. They stayed at roadside motels and made passionate love until they were exhausted. Together, they found true happiness and belonging.

After arriving at the family home on Brady Street, Ginger thoroughly charmed Parke's family. Mimi was disappointed at first to learn that the marriage was consummated without the benefit of a lavish wedding or their attendance, but it was unlike her to hold a grudge. Harry secretly enjoyed Parke making a decision that saved him money. They sent a photo and announcement to the *Quad-City Times,* a local newspaper, and invited friends and family to a reception at the country club the following Saturday. Ginger was a bit shy about what people would think of her deep, Southern accent. But the country club set accepted her with open arms and congratulations on "catching" Captain Parke Lusk.

The newlyweds found an apartment on Brady Street only blocks from Harry and Mimi's stately home. The apartment had a living room and kitchen-dining room on the first floor, with two bedrooms and a bath on the second floor. Both the living room and master bedroom had large windows looking out onto the tree-lined street. Though the apartment was perfectly suitable for the young couple, Parke missed his parents' sophisticated home and visited often. The big house made him feel safely embedded in the upper-class society and spoke to the image he wanted to portray. Comfortable rockers and porch swings on the wide, covered front porch were an ideal place to "be seen" by passersby.

Parke and Ginger did entertain at their apartment occasionally, inviting country club friends for drinks and dinner. In nice weather, the couples would sometimes walk to the public park rather than sit in the small backyard they shared with the family in the adjoining apartment. Both Parke and Ginger preferred socializing at the club where bartenders and waiters knew them by name and could deliver the perfect drinks to their table before they had barely sat down. It gave them a warm feeling of belonging. As Prohibition was still in force, the club could not sell alcohol, of course, but staff politely turned the other way as members discretely reached for their flasks to "fix" their cold beverage once delivered to the table. Alcohol was not difficult to come by and there was a vibrant underground industry to supply the need.

The country club was an extravagance that Parke considered basic livability. He loved golf, being part of the in-crowd, and especially the horses. He wanted that lifestyle for his family as well. Ginger was adept at making friends and she enjoyed the social life of the club, including playing cards, having drinks and dinner, and looking out over the well-maintained greens. Golf and horsemanship, however, were not her thing. Parke bought her numerous golf lessons, but just one riding lesson scared the hell out of her. Both attempts ended with her feeling humiliated in Parke's eyes.

"My lovely Ginger," he assured her. "I will be your knight in shining armor and rescue you on horseback as needed. All you need to do is be your perfect self."

With that, he would kiss her passionately on her red lips, making her swoon. Though she worried a bit that he might find formidable sporting women a distraction to their love, she tried hard not to show it. It was all clearly something very important to him, tied to his upbringing, and ingrained in his self-worth. She would support him in that. She hoped to impress him in other ways, such as with her Southern cooking filled with love, her quick wit and sense of humor, and her flare for adventure and fun. She prayed it would be enough.

For Parke, being part of the country club was about being accepted as a part of something bigger. It was a community built on shared appreciation of the finer things: membership by invitation only after voting by all the members. Admission meant you measured up to the higher standards of society. It spoke to Parke of his heritage, his right to belong, and his wish to receive honor.

Ginger had two deeply intertwined secrets. A baby boy had been born to Ginger when she was fifteen, resulting from a brief affair with a barnstormer who dazzled her with his daredevilry. Walter Gibbs was dashing in his helmet, goggles, and white scarf fluttering in the wind. He flew over her small hometown and, quite literally, swept her off her feet. This happened in Durant,

Mississippi, where her parents supplied everyone in town with dry goods from their first store. Their entire social life revolved around the Baptist church. When Ginger's stomach started to look as though she had swallowed a watermelon, her parents banished her in shame to a home for unwed mothers in Jacksonville. The child's adoption to eligible parents would follow.

Sadly, the baby boy did not survive his first hours of life outside the womb. It was a difficult birth and the child began to bleed from his umbilical cord. He suffered with a mysterious hereditary bleeding disorder. Baba spoke of the "weakness" only in muted whispers and vague references. There were stories about the time Myrtle's older brother, Tom, was stabbed and robbed by a desperate youth. And once there was an accident at the ammunition plant where he worked during the war. His grip slipped on a chisel driving it deep into the palm of his hand. His wife, mother, and sister took shifts at the hospital holding pressure bandages on the wound that would not stop bleeding. He led a sheltered life to avoid accidents. The affliction ran in the blood of the women of the family but only affected the boys.

After the death of Ginger's child born out of wedlock, the church turned their back on the Morgan family, asserting that they were introducing evil into the congregation. Well, they only knew the half of it. What Ginger, the attending doctor, and his nurse knew was that the baby had been as Black as Walter. Even though the community would never know this choice piece of damning gossip, her parents could not repair their family's reputation and they moved shortly thereafter to Hardenville, Missouri to begin again.

When Ginger first realized she was pregnant with Parke's child two years into their marriage, she told him about all this. Well, most of it. She spared him the color of the child. Together, they suffered through the gestation, hoping for a girl. If they did have a boy, they prayed he would somehow escape the hemophilia curse. She deeply regretted her forbidden affair with Walter. Parke was clearly the love of her life and her destiny. Parke and Ginger would snuggle in front of the evening fire, as he whispered sweet wishes to their unborn child. The birth of a healthy baby girl was a great relief to them. For decades, Parke continued to embellish the self-deprecating scene in the delivery room to everyone's delight.

Now, Parke and Ginger were entering the world of parenthood on their own after the leisurely recuperation in the hospital where Ginger enjoyed pampering with flowers, visitors, and many baby gifts, including a monogrammed silver cup and spoon from Mimi and Harry. It took Parke two trips in the Model A to get it all moved into their apartment. They named the new addition to the family Katherine, and shortened it to Kate within days.

Ginger started a baby book, lovingly kept in her first glow of motherhood. She wrote,

> *My darling baby girl smiled and even laughed to-*
> *day. She's pretty when she smiles, which is seldom.*

Another entry read,

Today, she took her first step at the age of nine months. Imagine that. So early. I think she's very smart for her age.

Though Parke made a decent income, Ginger was accustomed to being thrifty. She also needed projects to keep her mind and hands busy. She made little dresses from Parke's old shirts. The embroidery, tiny tucks, and smocking required hours at the ironing board. Parke worried when Kate did not eat. He would sit by her chair, trying to force spoons of mashed carrots and potatoes into her mouth, which came back out. Ginger did not worry.

"She'll eat if she's hungry. Leave her alone. She's just being stubborn. You're making her nervous," Ginger told Parke, but he persisted.

Little Kate was somber and assertive, not merry or smiley. She had very little hair, only a thin fringe at the nape of her neck. As she grew into a toddler, she would just as soon sit quietly turning the pages of picture books, rather than endure cuddling. Her favorite book was one of haiku poetry with magnificently delicate illustrations: the moon, a pair of graceful cranes, people walking in wooden, high sandals, and broad straw hats like umbrellas. Ginger would watch her staring at the foreign pictures and wonder what she was thinking. Her favorite toy was a Black doll given to her by a woman named Millie who took care of her at times. Millie's natural warmth and easy, relaxed affection were a soothing balm compared to Ginger's high-strung vibrations and Parke's over-indulgence.

Ginger referred to Millie as Katie's "mammy," a customary Southern term of the day for nanny. She pulled Kate and the precious doll in a red wagon the block-and-a-half to Vander Veer Park to play on the lawns and see the new, fluffy-yellow cygnets gliding in a shaded inlet of the lagoon. When she was one, some mysterious disease caused an angry rash and blinded her temporarily. Parke carried her around on a pillow so as not to irritate her inflamed skin.

"I haven't seen anything like this," the doctor told Parke. "There is so much we don't know. Pray for her and keep her as comfortable as you can. I will check back in a few days."

It took two weeks for her to recover. One of Parke's friends had a Kodak and posed Ginger and Kate for a photo just before she got sick. Kate sat on the porch railing at Mimi's house next to a large, potted primrose, with Ginger holding her from behind, wearing a cloche with a feather. Kate's booted foot soles pointed straight at the camera. Because of this photo, they decided Kate had "primrose rash."

Though the stock market crashed in 1929, its devastating effect had not quite made an impact on the Midwest. No one believed the economic indicators and the spirit of the Roaring Twenties prevailed. The new parents could afford some hired help, the club, socializing, and entertaining. They simply refused to listen. Oh, well, the elders were worried but not the young, married couples. They were still enjoying the exuberance of the Prohibition days, speakeasies, the age of flappers, jazz, the Charleston, bathtub gin, *Lady Chatterley's Lover*, and unconventional art. Before long, the impact did come.

By summer of 1930, prices were dropping and the brokerage business was suffering. Parke was becoming more worried every day at the news of growing unemployment, bank closures, and bread lines. The apartment in town was now too expensive for them.

Ginger said she wanted to move to the country "where we can live off the land, raise chickens, and have a garden." She grew up in a rural setting and felt comfortable with the whole idea. Her mother, raised on a farm, still kept a Jersey cow, chickens, and a large garden even after her marriage to a dry goods merchant. Parke knew nothing about farm life and was uneasy, but Ginger's enthusiasm gave him confidence. She was wild about the idea so they took long drives in the country looking for a new home.

There was a little farmhouse and ten acres for sale in Pleasant Valley on a bluff above the Mississippi River. It even had a barn. They found the property occupied by an old German widow, Mrs. Zantow. All her life she had toiled, from Germany emigrating to America and on to ranching in North Dakota living in a "soddy" while wheat fields waved around her. Life in Iowa had been easier, but then her husband died of typhoid. Now, she was tired. Her two grown sons left her alone in 1918 when Iowa Governor William L. Harding issued the Babel Proclamation forbidding people in the state from speaking any other language than English. Though her English was proficient, they had always spoken German at home and her accent was thick. The proclamation was an insult to their American patriotism. They begged their mother to give up on Iowa, but she would not leave the place where she had buried her husband. The boys went to Kansas City to avoid the animosity.

Parke and Ginger, with little Kate in tow, made many negotiating trips to the farm. The widow would insist that they have some summer sausage or homemade bread and she gave them crocks of churned, salted butter and eggs to take home. All this farm-plenty helped to Parke envisions himself as a gentleman farmer.

After some agonizing indecision and numerous persuasive arguments from Ginger, their declining income was the deciding factor. Finally, they made a deal to pay $30.00 a month toward the purchase of the small farm, which felt like heaven to Parke and Ginger. Parke found a little house in Bettendorf for Mrs. Zantow and on a golden, leaf-crunching day in September, they started a new life.

The four-room house had no running water or heat that first year. They carried water from an outside hand pump at the well and warmed the house with a smelly kerosene space heater and the kitchen wood stove. The move was undoubtedly the best thing they ever did.

Pleasant Valley

That first fall in Pleasant Valley, they celebrated with a Halloween housewarming. There was not much furniture and the floors were bare. Ginger raked leaves into the house to create an autumn carpet. She gathered cornstalks and a bale of straw from the neighboring farmer and covered all the bare lightbulbs with dark blue tissue paper lanterns and prepared two large punch bowls, one fruit and one with added spirits; rum, to be exact. Ginger and Dottie made a huge platter of little sandwiches with the crusts trimmed off and oranges were made into miniature jack-o-lanterns and filled with chocolate ice cream. There were pumpkins and decorative gourds laid about and the shed was transformed into a spook house where Parke told fortunes holding a flashlight under his face. It was dark and scary. Kate, going on three years old, complained that they did not have a *real* black cat.

All the relatives, plus a few neighbors, came to the party. Somehow, it became unclear which punch bowl was which. Teetotalers found themselves feeling quite giddy. It was a great get-together and a memorable beginning to the Pleasant Valley days of their lives—full of Ginger's enthusiasm, imagination, and witchcraft and Parke's magical charisma.

Ginger loved Christmas. She refused to have anything but the most beautiful Christmas tree. At Bechtel's Nursery, where she often went to talk with the owner's daughter, Liz, about plants, she picked out the evergreen in the field at the first sign of fall. The fir tree was marked with a bright red SOLD tag and she and Kate would visit it now and then to give words of encouragement and love. Once it was cut and delivered, they made decorations, painted walnuts and pinecones gold, found sprigs of bright-colored berries to dry, and cut out paper figures brought to life with crayons. There were not a lot of decorations, but the tree looked full and perfectly shaped, taking up a lot of space in their small house.

On Christmas Eve, they drove into Davenport to the Lusk family home on Brady Street. Decorated like a Christmas card, the house had evergreen garlands wrapped around the porch posts and paper bags with candles inside served as lanterns lining the walkway. Mimi had an enormous Christmas tree and festive candles burned everywhere. Aunt Dottie's family and Uncle Allen's family were all there and the cousins ran through the house playing with wild abandon. When it was time for dinner, everyone sat at the huge dining room table, even the smallest children, for a feast of ham, duck, roast beef, roasted potatoes, root vegetables, freshly-baked sage bread, and delectable desserts. Kate fell asleep on the way home wrapped in the warm embrace of that enchanting family gathering.

In the spring, Ginger gave birth to Margaret Ann, "Maggie. "Kate did not do well adjusting to the new arrival and Maggie's constant need for attention. One hot summer afternoon, Ginger put Kate down for her nap while continuing to play with the baby. Kate was angry and did not want a nap so she tore up the window shade, furiously ripping it to shreds. She received a sound spanking for her jealous rage. She never fully overcame her feeling of outrage toward Maggie, but after Kate realized her sister was here to stay, she came to accept her as an ally of sorts.

As the children grew, their world expanded to the outdoors. A cement walk, full of cracks, limped from the front to the back door and out to the driveway. A long hedge of snowy-white bridal wreath overflowed voluptuously down the drive to the road. The rest of the property was fenced off for a cow pasture, which included ancient twisted apple trees from what was once an orchard. An old barn presided at the top of the drive. At one end was a dirt floor garage. The rest of the barn was for chickens. A ladder led up to a loft where some pigeons roosted. Next to the barn was a red-slatted corncrib and the old outhouse with two holes.

Pleasant Valley was a little spot in the road with a train depot, a grocery store (without much food), a post office (in the grocery store), a tavern, and onions. The black soil of the Mississippi River Valley was famous for its onion fields. In the summer at harvest-time, the predominant odor was onion—strong onion. People who worked in the fields would come into the store bearing a formidable stench. You could drive from Bettendorf to Pleasant Valley, about eight miles, and the aroma was practically shimmering on the air like a mirage.

Their house was a quarter mile from the small general store where a narrow-gauge train stopped daily to deliver mail and freight. Kate dreamed of the dreadful black behemoth roaring closer and closer, chasing her with its snarling cowcatcher teeth chomping at her heels. *CHUF, CHUF, Chufchufchufchufchuf.* Her screams were silent and she woke with a gasp. This nightmare alternated with one about a mayonnaise jar caught in bedsprings. The dream made no sense, but after all it is not what happens in a dream but how you feel about it. For Kate it was a nightmare.

Eventually, the vicious smoke-billowing steam engine and the seemingly scary bedsprings vanished to be replaced by pony and flying dreams. Parke instigated the flying dreams with his elaborate bedtime stories. Then he rubbed Vaseline on their shoulder blades so they could grow wings.

Meanwhile, Ginger had major sewing days with her friend, Clara Bell, Adele's mother. While they stitched away, the kids played "'tend like," a game of imagination in which they pretended to be someone else. Adele skipped and danced across the lawn, flailing her arms and proclaiming her intentions to become a movie star. Kate wanted to be a cowboy. Little Maggie followed them around dragging toys behind her.

The sewing days involved an assembly line construction of underpants, nightgowns, slips, and identical Dotted Swiss dresses for the three
girls. As with everything that Ginger undertook, her sewing was to excess. Grandiose results. No feeble enterprises.

Every summer, a caravan of gypsy wagons camped in a shady edge of the fields to stay for harvesting and then they would move on, working their way south before winter wielded its heavy hand. Kate always wanted to see the gypsies. They seemed to live a romantic life, with their horses and colorful wagons, and she imagined they wore large gold earrings and bright skirts when dancing in the firelight.

Down on the riverbank, there was a campground with cabins, a small stand selling pop, and a dock over the swirling brown water. At times, the strong current tried to sweep the girls away as they held tight to Parke's outstretched arms. He forbid them to go near the river without his parental supervision. The girls imagined that the murky waters harbored hideous snapping fish, in addition to the all-too-real charging monster logs and the broken glass in the muddy bottom. But when it is 106 degrees in the river humidity, the cooling waters were the only respite. A neighbor helped Parke build a summer kitchen off the back porch to keep the cooking and laundry heat out of the house.

Their house had once been an Indian trading post. The dining room still had the original hand-hewn beams. Behind this room was a bedroom where they all slept, until a dividing wall made two bedrooms. A kitchen was on one side and a living room on the other. They made gradual improvements on the little house, including a bathroom and an oil burner they named Leo the Lion. He was big and black and lived with an enormous bull snake in a hole dug out of the yellow clay under the house. He made a comfortable purring noise and blew hot air up through the registers placed in the floor. The outhouse remained even after the bathroom installation and it continued to inspire jokes. Parke told stories about it. "Once upon a time, there were two little girls named Kate and Maggie who woke up early on a snowy morning and ran fast to the outhouse with a bear (bare) behind."

Every morning, about 7:00, Parke left for work. In the summer, Kate and Maggie sprang from their bed when they heard the car engine turning over and ran naked out to the fence to wave goodbye as he passed down the road. Morning glories covered the fence and they squatted to pee into the flowers as they waved and shouted, "Bring us presents!"

Every evening at 5:30, Parke arrived home from the office. The girls screamed with delight at the sound of the engine a quarter mile away. He might have dripping ice cream cones or a dime store trinket like a tiny celluloid doll or a rubber ball. These items were hidden in the house and the girls played "hot and cold" to find them. You were hot when near the item and cold when you looked in the wrong place. Once, he brought home a cardboard box with three gum wrappers in it. Then, with magic words and flourishes, the gum wrappers transformed into three fluffy-white kittens. No one ever figured out how he did this. It was the best surprise of all.

Kate started school in the fall of 1933. Ginger made cotton print dresses with matching bloomers. She pinned a handkerchief to Kate's dress and Parke drove her to the schoolhouse on his way to work, where Kate insisted on tripping up the walk by herself in brand new brown leather shoes. Tears came to Parke's eyes as he observed his baby girl marching so bravely into the world.

On one day of the following spring, they all drove to Buffalo, Iowa, a town five miles west of Davenport on the river, to see Clara, her husband Collie, and Adele. They lived in a house without a kitchen so they used the one in the house next door that belonged to Collie's father, who abandoned it in favor of living on the river in a houseboat. He was once a riverboat captain. The Bell's house was in a wooded, isolated spot up a rutty dirt road and under construction—in the dream stage—to include a large, high-ceilinged living room and bedrooms upstairs.

The grown-ups were content to sip their drinks, getting loudly intoxicated and imagining they were having witty conversations. The three children created a play. It started in the woods as they rode astride downed trees galloping through the forest, shooting at each other, dying with great flair, and coming back to life.

Adele wanted a romantic dancing role. "I'll be Natashia. You, Kate, be the prince and Maggie is the cruel mother, see? So, I run through the woods dancing," she directed and then skipped off, disappearing from their sight. Kate tried getting in the princely mood by picking up a stick and feigning sword fighting while Maggie sat on a stump frowning up a cruel mother face but failing to think up any other action for her role.

Adele did not come back for a long time. "Let's find her," Kate urged, but Maggie had to pee and ran to the house. Kate was still looking for Adele when Maggie came back. The woods were eerily quiet, evoking visions of lurking danger. A crow cawed and they jerked; a twig snapped and they stopped to listen. Kate hit a tree with her stick sword—a show of bravado. Maggie seemed oblivious in her nonchalant manner—only four and clearly in control. She followed behind Kate, entirely focused on her cruel mother character, but saying nothing. As far as she was concerned, total concentration was all that was required for her role.

About this time, Adele appeared suddenly before them outraged, her tiny, pointed face red with fury. "You're supposed to chase me!" she screamed. "Where were you? Don't you *stupids* know how to play? Kate, you must act like the prince who is in love with me. You come find me, take me in your arms, and kiss me, like this. And, Maggie, you get mad and yell at the prince to go away, get it?"

"Well, how can I come find you when I don't know where you are? You know these woods. We've never been here before," Kate shot back.

Adele tossed her blond curls and haughtily stomped off, showing much disdain for the two "stupids."

Maggie built their pony dreams with stories about Tom Mix riding over the hill from the West to bring them ponies. Kate's fine white-blonde hair turned strawberry-blonde as she grew. Maggie's was a thick golden blonde. The sisters sat side-by-side on the hill, their braids hanging down their backs like loose tethers, straining their eyes to the next hill where the sun set. They could see the riders coming, created out of the tombstones of the cemetery. The sun glancing off the white stones and the shadows of windblown trees made them gallop. Kate and Maggie talked themselves into a thrilling, vicarious gleeful experience—shaking, laughing, stomach-clutching. Even though they both totally believed with all their hearts that Tom Mix was on his way from the West to bring them ponies—Kate's was black with a white mane and tail and Maggie's was white with a black mane and tail—they did not come. Maggie told stories that made Kate laugh and cry and believe in miracles.

Kate and Maggie made dolls out of hollyhock flowers and cooked mud pies into hard cakes in the hot sun. They fed the dolls huge clay plates of catalpa "beans," ran through the spray from the hose, and went without clothing much of the time in their relatively remote yard. One time they received invitations to a birthday party and Ginger planned to doll them up in new yellow calico dresses. That morning, Ginger gave them proper baths, including making them suffer the outrage of hair washing. While Ginger was preparing a gift basket of little surprises to take to the party, the girls decided to become Indians. After all, Ginger always laughed and teased about how they were growing up "like wild Indians," running naked all summer.

Under the box elder trees, the girls discovered a good mud puddle in the clay. They started methodically covering their entire bodies with the brown ooze. When they were completely unrecognizable as normal four- and six-year-old White children, they ran to the kitchen door and knocked.

"Look, we're Indians!" they shouted in glee.

Ginger did not laugh, but she silently congratulated herself on waiting to put them in their dresses until it was time to get in the car. She knew her kids. However, she did have to call Liz Bechtel to explain that the girls would be late to the party.

When Maggie was five and Kate was seven, they embarked on a forbidden adventure. There was a gate across the bottom of the driveway to keep them in the yard, marking their boundary. Across the road, there was a family, with two girls their same ages. They would occasionally play with them but not often. Kate and Maggie usually played by themselves, but the urge to socialize overcame Kate one day. She coerced Maggie into crawling under the gate first, who then ran across the road. When the coast was clear, Kate followed and once together again, their skinny legs flew down the road to the neighbor's driveway. Much to everyone's embarrassment, the neighbor kids were taking naps. Their mother called Ginger, who came to collect her miscreants. While walking back home she looked furious. She was thinking up a suitable punishment. There were weeping willow trees in their yard so a willow switch was the weapon of choice. Maggie received the first sting on the legs because Kate was keeping her distance. Maggie pulled away from Ginger and both girls started running. Around and around the barn they sped with exceptional inspiration and Ginger close behind. Soon, however, they were all out of breath and Ginger started laughing helplessly. She had a hard time administering tough punishment.

On another hill, behind their house, lived a family who must have been rich. The Tanners had two houses: a yellow, brick house for the wife and a brown, wood-framed home for the husband. In the valley between their two houses, there was a small farmhouse and a barn where their caretaker lived. In the barn was a large Palomino jumping horse. Kate and Maggie knew he could jump because he often soared over the fence to arrive on a misty morning in their orchard, happily munching apples.

They also had a black-and-white Pinto pony and employed a real cowboy named Dodie Fields—bowlegs and all. Parke got along well with Dodie, as he did with everyone. His friends ranged from the professionals he encountered through his work, to the Black man who polished shoes at the street corner, to a retired rodeo clown, and to a hundred-year-old man who lived in a one-room shack. Dodie brought the pony, Jackie, to visit the girls sometimes. The kind gesture, however, did not fulfill their dreams of having their own, as Parke hoped it would. As a consolation, Dodie taught the girls to stand on their heads.

Imaginative Ginger envisioned their farm surrounded with gardens and lawn. She would eventually landscape a good portion of the property, but first she started with the dump ravine, which ran lengthwise down a slope with a willow at the foot and a copse of box elder at the top. Long-dead tools and junk had transformed the ravine from a clean vessel to a rusted pit begging for love. Some men came clanging into the yard one day with a team of huge draft horses and hauled out the old carcass of a car, along with years of miscellaneous tin cans, bottles, enameled pans, and metal parts.

Given Iowa's grave economic conditions in 1933, it was not a time to be running out and buying bedding plants. Ginger found boulders beside the road to plant on the two slopes of her rock garden so they looked as if they had merely emerged from the settlement of the earth. As she formed the landscape, small nooks and miniature garden spots evolved inviting the placement of a wild flower here, a fern or dwarf shrub there, until all felt like a fairyland. In fact, under a shelf rock, which formed a small cave, Twinkie lived. She was a personal fairy belonging to the family.

The sisters would often "go to the woods" with Ginger and Twink to find plants for the fairyland. There were violets, daisies, bluebells, cornflowers, wild asters, yellow dogtooth violets, Johnny Jump-ups, delicate white Queen Anne's lace, pink phlox, shooting stars, columbine, bleeding hearts, evening primrose, gold and red coreopsis, black-eyed Susans, dandelions, blue flax, morning glories, and may apples. Maggie liked to work close beside Ginger, but Kate was usually off in her own dream world, taking it all in, arranging in her mind the fantastic transformation.

Twink was a product of Parke's storytelling, which made their lives so rich. She had the ability to turn a fence post into anything one's heart desired. Sometimes though, she would make a mistake and, instead of a pony, they would get a goat, or instead of a beautiful ballerina costume, they would get a clown suit. However, it was all okay because the main purpose of the story was to entertain and stimulate imagination. Even sad stories were acceptable and could become fun, because when a baby kitten fell off the bridge and broke her little paw, limping and crying, Twink would come along to mend the poor little kitty with a wave of her wand.

Despite their financial situation, Ginger traded her sewing skills to pay for the girls to take tap and acrobatic lessons. She helped them practice the dances by playing an imaginary piano and humming the tunes, *East side, West side, All around the town*, and *Just tea for two and two for tea*. The teacher's name was Mr. Telke. His breath smelled like coffee. Ginger made black satin tap pants and long-sleeved white satin blouses for Christmas. They wore the outfits when Parke took the family out to dinner at a dark, gloomy second-rate restaurant. He made an arrangement or some sort of trade with the owner for a free dinner. Soon after, they had to stop the lessons.

By this time, Parke was having trouble making the mortgage payments on their house. He still had sales, but they were growing smaller as his clients lacked the capital to stock their shelves. One of Mrs. Zantow's sons, Will, moved back from Kansas City and rented a small house down the hill. His mother would come out to visit him often and they all enjoyed seeing the brusque German woman with the deep accent and kind heart. Whenever he could, Parke sent the girls to Will's place with a $30.00 house payment check. Parke and Ginger stopped going to the country club and were often "on the wagon" without the resources to purchase alcohol. His white dress shirts frayed at the collar and cuffs.

There was a small grocery store next to the Union Bank Building that housed the brokerage office. Ginger called Parke each day to talk about what to get for dinner. For a while, the grocer allowed a charge account, but one day he refused to put any more purchases on credit. Ginger had to be creative in inventing meals out of what Parke could buy. Weekly staples included vegetable soup from the garden's bounty; baked beans with hamburger; homemade sauerkraut and German sausages from Mrs. Zantow; and a rice dish with onions, canned tomatoes, and fried bacon bits that Ginger named Rice Dang-Dang to make it sound fancy. When she added fresh herbs from the garden, she really could make these dishes tasty. Bread that was not entirely consumed when fresh became an after-dinner surprise of bread pudding. By then, they had adopted a St. Bernard named Buck, which was another big appetite to feed. Parke brought him home because the owner could no longer feed the large dog. Ginger often fed Buck oatmeal with a little meat drippings mixed in.

In these lean years, the girls learned remarkable resilience through Parke and Ginger's creativity. The vegetable gardens and chickens fed them, but it was Ginger's flower garden and Parke's stories that tended their souls.

Eventually, Parke swallowed his pride and borrowed money from his brother, Allen, who, in addition to managing the business' finances, had married the daughter of a bank president. Parke would never dream of even asking his father. Harry was clear with the boys at an early age that he would not support them beyond college. They were to make their own way in the world. One day, they would inherit money from him, but that was all. Allen was smug about his accomplishments and a bit jealous of Parke's popularity. Allen mercilessly razzed Parke about his ragged shirts. Once, he even grabbed the shirt on Parke's back, ripping it down the middle. He thought this was hilarious, but Parke was deeply humiliated. These lean days had their permanent impact in many ways. They changed Parke from a cheerful, happy person to one with a furrowed brow.

To keep from worrying and wishing he had a drink, Parke brought home several books from the library in the evening and read until 1:00 in the morning. Sometimes, if they had enough sugar, he would go to the kitchen with his book to perch on a stool by the stove and make a treat. Fudge was one of his favorites. You could always tell whether it was a good book or not. If it was absorbing, the fudge became rock fudge. If it was a lousy book, he grew impatient and removed the candy from the burner too soon. That batch became a soupy fudge eaten on crackers. After many spells of bad fudge, Ginger finally came to the rescue with a recipe from the newly published and highly acclaimed *Joy of Cooking* she found at the library for the finest, creamiest confection ever.

Tramps came along the highway on their long hikes to look for work. They were gaunt, quiet, and disparaging. Sometimes, out of sheer desperation, they would knock at the back door and ask politely and quietly, with hat in hand, if Ginger had anything to spare. She gave the men fried eggs and bread to be eaten at the end of the sidewalk. Parke was afraid for Ginger living isolated in the country, but she could not turn them down and was sure these men were harmless. She never refused when they came to the door, but she did impose new rules about the kids being fully clothed no matter the temperature. The sisters watched these men from behind a tree. Ginger told the girls to stay away; not because the men were dangerous but because the girls would embarrass them with the eager friendliness so natural in well-loved children. Mostly, they were shy and humble men in clean overalls.

There was talk of the U.S. Army Corps of Engineers building a lock and dam in Davenport, which would put hundreds to work. Improvements were going on all up and down the Mississippi River as the government designed work projects to aid in navigation, flood control, rural electrification, and employment for men. Everyone held on, waiting for the project to get fully underway and bring much-needed income into the local economy.

The county fair provided respite from their worries during these years. The family would spend an entire day looking at all the livestock and watching the competitions. Ginger entered her raspberry jam and blueberry peach pie and Dodie did trick riding presentations.

One year, the Ringling Bros. and Barnum & Bailey Circus came to town. Kate wanted to go so badly that she smashed her favorite horse bank with a hammer to get out the money. It turned out there was only eighty-three cents in it, which was not enough.

Circus day came and Kate had not heard any discussion about going. Parke went to the office in the morning, as usual, and by the time he came home for lunch, Kate was making herself sick to her stomach for feeling left out. Finally, after he finished his lunch, he said, "Okay—let's go to the circus!" Everyone jumped up and down and screamed with joy. Kate really did not know what to expect a circus to be like. The posters had a tiger jumping through a hoop of fire and an elephant, but the excitement of experiencing the unknown made her head throb. It probably did not help that she had refused both breakfast and lunch. Ginger made her drink a tall glass of cool water and take some deep breaths. On their way to the circus, they stopped at a bakery store, where Parke hoped to make a sale. The man had hot roasted peanuts and he gave Maggie and Kate each a small bag for the elephants.

When they finally entered the gates, saw the crowds of people, heard the noise of the pipe organ, and the barker calling out the sideshows, Kate's appetite came back. She started cracking open the warm peanuts. Parke bought them pink cotton candy to stick their faces into. The barker raved about all the enticing oddities they could see inside and Parke counted his change to see if he had enough for all of them to go in. Once inside, they saw the "fat lady" and some dwarfs. Kate felt embarrassed for them sitting up on a platform. Nobody talked to them. There was a rubber man who could put a dozen golf balls in his mouth and a two-headed baby, depicted outside as a real live baby, playing ball, but it was really a dead baby in a jar. The best part was a man carrying around a board covered with chameleons. Each one had a tiny delicate chain around its neck with a safety pin at the end, so you could wear it on your chest for a decoration.

After the sideshow, they went to the menagerie to see lions, tigers, horses, camels, giraffes, zebras, and, best of all, the elephants, who raised their trunks to accept the peanuts the girls dropped in the holes above the bins. Their thick ankles, held by shiny brass bracelets chained to stakes in the ground, were supposed to keep them from wandering around tearing things up and terrorizing people.

"Daddy, I can't believe those tethers can really hold on to those elephants," Kate said.

"No, honey, they can't," Parke told her. "They are just there to make the visitors feel safer. It's on the honor system. The elephants are part of the circus family and don't want anything more right now than your peanuts."

In the Big Top, the show began with a parade led by the clowns and strutting aerialists and acrobats, followed by the animals. Kate's heart was racing and tears were leaking from her eyes. It was all just too much for kids who lived a quiet existence in the country. When the elephants, who came last, went by with the glittering ladies riding astride their necks, rocking back and forth, Kate decided to become a circus performer instead of a cowboy.

Performances began simultaneously in the three rings and it was impossible to see everything. There were amazing balancing acts, which they later tried at home, the flying trapeze artists, a man was shot from a cannon, and African women publicized as "Ubangi Savages" with plates in their lips, rode by on a flatbed. Another float carried women from Burma who wore gold rings on their necks, to make them grow longer. The rings were to protect them from tiger attacks and did not stretch the neck but instead pushed down their collarbones and ribs. It made their heads look too small.

The very best of all was Clyde Beatty, the lion tamer. The roustabouts constructed a round cage in the center ring. Then out came the man in white riding pants and black boots wearing a holster and pistol and carrying a long whip. With much shouting and whip cracking, he made the lions and tigers sit on stools and jump through flaming hoops and he put his head in a lion's mouth. Once, when his back was turned, a tiger lunged after him and an assistant outside the ring shot his pistol in the air. The skilled assistant had to enter the ring to help get the big cat back under control. Then Kate and Maggie finally took a breath.

When it was all over, Kate had to have a little whip, sold by a huckster on the way out. Buck suffered many humiliations when he became the brunt of attempts to master lion taming. He was a good-natured dog who put up with kids sitting on him to tie their shoes or attempt to ride him at a gallop across the yard. His skin was too loose so they always fell off. Once, they tied him to a small table in the living room while he played the role of the horse. When someone came to the kitchen door, he ran, crashing and banging all the way through the house, dragging the table behind.

Another time, Parke had a harness made for hitching him to a goat cart. Buck patiently let them attach him to the wagon. They climbed onto the seat, but he would not move. There they sat, yelling at him and trying to lead him, but he stood frozen. About that time, a car drove up the driveway and Buck suddenly took off running, slamming the cart from one side to the other, against trees and fences and reducing the thing to splinters.

Ginger went about performing the incredibly tedious jobs of cleaning, cooking, washing, and ironing. Ironing went on forever. For entire days, she stood over the hot ironing board and still the basket was not empty. An old trunk became a receptacle for items waiting in need of pressing. The shirts and dresses piled up; favorites often ironed at the last minute. Everything required ironing.

While she ironed, she played the radio, listening to soapbox operas telling their mundane stories of ordinary people like Ma Perkins. She derived some consolation from hearing about their problems, but eventually Ginger began having trouble relating to these make-believe people. She felt different. Her senses were easily aroused to the point of soaring by symphonic music, beautiful paintings, dramatic literature, and kind words. Discontentment started setting in and she had to dig deep to shrug it off.

Sometimes, Ginger's emotional state dissolved into uncontrollable weeping. She would collapse on the bed and refuse to eat or change her clothes. She would ignore the children. Kate made peanut butter sandwiches for her and Maggie. They would sit on the knoll, eat their sandwiches, and look off down the road waiting to see Daddy's car. Ginger worried about Parke, about money, and she dwelled on the loss of her first child. Eventually, the storm passed. Ginger would rise to be her blithe, spirited self and play with the children again. Well, mostly with Maggie. She was a merry little one. Sibling rivalry emerged inevitably and fierce anger exploded from Kate who stabbed her little sister in the forehead with a pencil. Maggie retaliated by sticking Kate in the wrist with the scissors.

Parke smoothed things over with stories. One was about Tallulah.

Once upon a time, there was a big, brown wild turkey. She was so wild that no human being had ever seen her because she always hid in the woods. Her name was Tallulah and she was this big (holding his hands about three feet above the floor). She had a particularly bright red waddle. It was very appealing.

One day, she fell in love, built a nest, and laid seventeen eggs. Unfortunately, snakes and skunks gobbled up most of them. However, five eggs did hatch into the most beautiful babies she had ever seen, so she named them after famous people. Tennessee, Twain, Tarkington, and Tennyson because she liked names that started with T. She named the fifth one Faulkner because he was a little odd.

Soon, they grew big enough to graze with her. They walked back and forth across a big pasture from woods to woods. Back and forth and back and forth.

At the edge of the woods, there was a house. A man, known only as Seth, set out cracked corn on a board in the back yard for the birds. Early one morning, when all was quiet, Tallulah took Tennessee, Twain, Tarkington, Tennyson, and Faulkner to the bird feeder for a wonderful breakfast.

All summerlong, the babies walked across the pasture, eating grasshoppers and growing big. Almost as big as their mother.

Then, one frosty morning, Seth heard turkey gobbling all around the house. It was strange. Usually, turkeys stayed away from the house because they were afraid of people.

Seth looked out the window. He saw a big turkey on the patio. It was Tallulah. Her head and tail drooped and she looked sick. Her feathers were ruffled. Her eyes looked bleary and dull. She heard her flocks' urgent clucking and she remembered when they were tiny, fluffy babies. Her head popped up. She saw them at the bird feeder nearby.

Her long red legs struggled to lift her body. She dragged her feet across the yard to join the flock. All together for the last time, they pecked at the cracked corn until they were full.

Then Tennessee, Twain, Tarkington, Tennyson, and Faulkner paraded bravely out across the pasture. Tallulah watched them go and she shuffled, stumbled, and staggered off into the woods to go to the big turkey shoot in the sky.

By the time Parke came to the part about Tallulah remembering when her chicks were babies, tears were streaming down the girls' cheeks. At the end, they were sobbing and blowing noses. Parke threw back his head and laughed, satisfied with his ability to evoke emotion. He jollied them around and changed the subject until they were laughing, but it did not erase the image.

Grandmothers

THE NEXT SUMMER, IN 1935, Ginger took Maggie on the train to Mississippi to visit relatives and Parke and Kate stayed with Mimi and Harry for a while. Will Zantow agreed to feed Buck and the chickens during their absence. Times were rough and taking a toll on Parke and Ginger's marriage. Parke stayed out late many evenings, leaving Kate alone with Mimi. Aunt Dottie and her children lived nearby and visited sometimes so Kate had someone to play with. Kate heard her daddy come in during the night and saw him go down the hall to the bathroom, naked, muttering to himself. Mimi suggested Kate draw a picture of him when she was feeling blue and lonely. She drew a picture of him naked. Mimi was shocked and spoke to Parke about that.

Mimi never wore a corset, donned sloppy dresses, and did not care if her slip hemline showed or her stockings sagged. When she went out, she wore flamboyant, big hats in the summer and fluffy, furry-collared coats in the winter. Her bedroom had a dresser full of powder puffs, perfumes, jewelry, and the inevitable handkerchief hung to dry plastered to the mirror. She enjoyed lolling on her pillows. She ordered the maid, or her daughter, to bring a tray of tea with lots of sugar cubes and maybe some sugar wafer cookies. Sometimes, they had ginger ale instead. She would spend time chatting with her grandkids and always found what they thought and said entertaining. Mimi let Kate wear perfume and use the powder puff to powder her nose. They took turns reading passages from the Bible aloud. "God is Love," Mimi proclaimed and burned incense in little ceramic monkeys inscribed "Hear no evil, see no evil, speak no evil." Mimi was outrageous and fun!

Harry had become a quiet man, in contrast to his younger years, and spent hours playing solitaire when he was not at work. Mimi asked the kids not to bother him and, in turn, he did not initiate any interaction with them. He had a Victrola and played quarter-inch-thick Caruso recordings in the evenings after dinner. It was Mimi, rather than Harry, who raised her brood to have a sense of humor and be cheerful. Every gathering at their grandparents' house was full of warmth, silliness, and laughter, observed by Harry but without his participation. His business was his world and his legacy. The poor economy was making it difficult for him to maintain the life he wanted to provide for his family. He took it personally, feeling that he should be able to rise above and succeed regardless of the damned national economic conditions.

Harry and Parke had a cordial relationship, but it was clear, even for young Kate, that they were not close. Harry found Parke to be too generous and easy going as a father. He sometimes found Parke to be somewhat effeminate with his big friendly smile and silly jokes. Harry believed in macho dominance in business and marriage. He thought Ginger sweet at first, but the more he knew her, he suspected she was raising the girls to be too strong willed; these were unflattering qualities in young "ladies." He preached to Parke that the girls would need to go to finishing school to make their way successfully in society.

Parke thought about this and talked to his mother about it. Mimi advised, "Well, that certainly will not hurt Kate and Maggie. At some point, they will become whoever they truly are. But you still have some time to influence their intellect and spirit."

Parke decided he would discuss this with Ginger to see what she thought. It was difficult to imagine a time when Kate would come of age but never too early to start making plans for the future.

In a few weeks, when Ginger and Maggie came back, Parke found that Maggie had learned to recite some Negro Dialect poems, an emerging genre of the time, handed down by some of Ginger's family friends in Mississippi. Kate was quite jealous of all the attention her sister received when she stood up to perform.

> *Ah bin goin' to Sunday school, To git in on da tree,*
> *But look what ole Santy Claus Pulled off and give*
> *ta me. Ah wanted a train o' cars Dat run on a*
> *track, But he give me a sour orange An' a dumb*
> *ole jumpin' jack.*

There was no doubt that Ginger would eventually come back. Those early years in the country with no running water and scanty income to make improvements were difficult. Besides, she missed her native Mississippi and sometimes yearned for a return to the ways of her childhood. A Black mammy raised and thoroughly spoiled her. Ginger spent much time playing with her mammy's children at their home, which was not far from her own. They lived in the small town of Kosciusko near the scenic Yockanookany River. Large terrapin, big enough to ride on, lived in their backyard. She brought North with her a deepened Southern drawl and food such as yams, turnips, mustard greens cooked in ham fat, corn bread, and grits. The Lusks raised Parke on bland English beefy foods. Mimi never learned to cook, which made her servants a necessity for survival.

Mimi had a cook, Ellie, and a housekeeper named Agnes, both in their mid-twenties. Agnes lived in the attic, while Ellie arrived each morning at 6:00 to make breakfast. When they gathered for breakfast, Mimi would ask Harry what he preferred for dinner, which he rarely acknowledged. Afterwards, Ellie would meet with Mimi in the kitchen to plan the other meals of the day. Ellie shopped for fresh food at the market and cooked the sorts of things Mimi had grown up on: beef and potatoes, roasted pork with turnips and carrots, Shepherd's pie, Chicken Divan, poached fish and rice. On occasion, Mimi would suggest something daring she had heard about or read in *Ladies Home Journal*, such as *tetrazzini* or baked macaroni and cheese, to which Harry would grumble, "No meat?" Ellie was a competent cook and her rotund physique spoke to her own love of food. Nonetheless, she was limited to what Mimi thought desirable.

Agnes spent her days cleaning and doing laundry and, thus, was thin from climbing stairs all day. Sometimes, Agnes helped

Ellie in the kitchen or with serving, especially when Mimi planned a party or there was a special event such as a birthday. Oysters came up on the riverboats and the simple, yet sophisticated, Oysters Rockefeller was a favorite for special events. Agnes had Mondays off, while Ellie had Thursdays off. On Wednesdays, Ellie cooked ahead for the following day and instructed Agnes how to rewarm or finish the dinner recipe.

Clifford was the gardener. He worked one or two days a week, depending on the season, mowing, watering, pruning, planting, and raking leaves.

By September, Parke and Ginger were together again at the farm in Pleasant Valley, when Ginger received a telegram that her father had died unexpectedly of a heart attack. She wept and felt guilty her recent trip had been to Mississippi rather than Missouri to see her beloved parents. Concerned about the economy and her ability to go it alone, Baba sold off the remainder of the store goods and left the rented house in Hardenville to live with her daughter's family. The summer kitchen was enclosed and made into a bedroom for her. She brought with her two feather beds in a freight car. One of the mattresses replaced the old saggy one shared by Kate and Maggie. Fluffing up the feather bed was a big job requiring all hands to make it full and luxurious. The girls took turns standing on the rail at the foot of the bed and falling backwards into the bed, engulfed in cozy feathers.

When Baba arrived, Ginger relinquished a good part of raising the children to her. Ginger worked more in the garden during the week, but on Friday, she cleaned herself up, fixing her hair, giving herself a manicure, shaving her legs—the works.

Parke might stop at the Pleasant Valley Tavern on his way home from work for a drink with the fellas and then pick up Ginger to go out. Out most often meant by themselves, on a date, driving around, parking, talking, dreaming, and necking. The date sometimes lasted all weekend. During the week, they would both sit up late every night, reading and fixing midnight snacks like sardines on crackers, or *oeufs au beurre noir*.

The girls were home with Baba one evening and she was making iron toast by smashing a slice of Wonder bread flat and crisp with a clothes iron. A boiling mountain of clouds came grumbling down the steaming river at the brink of night. It was that mystical time between the glow of sun and the depths of sleep. There was a distant thunder and the room grew darker. Kate and Maggie were tired and full of iron toast. Baba was trying to entertain them by talking about how her mother could make objects move with her mind. She said it was "electricity." After much urging and begging the girls persuaded her to try it.

A table was to be the object; not a rickety card table but a solid, twenty-one- by eighteen-inch mahogany table with a drawer in it. They put it in the middle of the floor and pulled up three chairs. Baba instructed Maggie and Kate to place their hands lightly on the table's surface alongside Baba's hands. Their fingers touched to form a circle, thumb-to-thumb and pinky-to-pinky. "Be quiet and concentrate," Baba ordered. The room grew darker.

Kate tried to concentrate but felt suspicious of possible trickery and kept glancing down to check on Baba's knees, which might be able to lift the table. Baba closed her eyes and began drawling in long, drawn out tones, "Rise... table... rise, rise...

table... rise," repeatedly. It seemed to go on for a long time and Baba contorted her face with terrible effort.

Eventually, there was a tiny shudder of the table. The girl's heavy-lidded eyes flew open. Then, it settled squarely again. Baba cautioned them to *concentrate*. The table rose again. They all pushed back their chairs. The table spun in a slow circle on one leg as they all maintained their light touch and followed it around. The girl's hearts were pounding with excitement and wonder. Finally, the object of their intense concentration settled down. Baba heaved a huge sigh and appeared rather faint and weak, as though the ordeal had drained her strength.

Baba explained that psychokinetic powers are only possible in a room of believers. Baba, Maggie and Kate *did* believe and the world of spirits came alive for them. Maggie and Kate worked on the magic with a playmate, Charlotte, who also wanted to believe. After long spells of "rise... table... rise" sessions with no results, they finally resorted to learning how to play the ukulele. This amounted mostly to "My dog has fleas" tuning up and one song:

> *Quitcha', quitcha', quitcha', quitcha lookin'*
> *around, making them eyes at the men. Ainta'*
> *bita', bita', bita', bita' lady-like, don't ya' let me*
> *catch ya' at it again.*

When the girls talked with Ginger about the table rising incident later, she looked down at the floor, nodded her head ever so slightly, and assumed a knowing look. It seemed to the girls that their mother knew, full well, about Baba's powers and that it was a sacred family secret. When they told Parke about it, he looked up at the ceiling with a thoughtful, wistful look that made them think he was not a believer but that he wanted to know how she did it. Party tricks were his specialty. When Charlotte talked to her own parents about all this, they suspected witchcraft and only let her play with Kate and Maggie under their direct supervision thereafter.

Baba was a lousy cook, according to Ginger who liked to try fancy new recipes, but she took cake baking seriously. She made her cakes from scratch, mixed them with her bare hands, never read a recipe, and used lavishly rich ingredients. They were the best! Back in Mississippi, social life meant a big competition for the winning cake brought to a "dinner on the ground" gathering. She usually won, although a certain Miz Tuttle could also make a mean cake.

The only other food that Baba truly excelled at making was fried chicken. The most important prerequisites were the correct size and the "home grownness." Fryer size must be about two pounds, young, tender, and a bit spindly. One of the gleefully choice moments of this ritual was the "ringing of the necks." Kate and Maggie ran around to catch the chickens and deliver them to Baba, who would ring their necks to make them stop struggling and then lay them on a stump to chop their heads off. The girls watched with horrible fascination as the headless bodies flopped all over the ground for an unbelievably long time. Just when you thought they had finally given up the ghost, FLOP—there they went again.

After they were quiet for good, Baba dipped them in a tub of scalding hot water and plucked all the feathers. Then she singed them with a great torch of twisted newspaper, making a nasty stench, and plunged them in the kitchen sink to pull the guts out with her bare hands. The birds were soaked in cold salt water and cut up properly. No butcher could ever do justice to the dissection of a fryer like her. No chopping and whacking here. She carefully separated each joint. Best of all, the wishbone was carefully saved as a separate piece.

After all the work, the family gathered at the dinner table, where Parke always served the meat. He had all the plates stacked up and he fixed the children's, asking which piece each wanted. Then he asked Baba what she wanted and much to everyone's annoyance, she always said, "Oh, I'll just take the back." After all that work!

She was so humble, polite, and neat. She made her own clothes by the same perfectly fitting dress pattern, which she had also made herself. She wore a full corset—summer and winter. She never wanted more than two dresses per season. A housedress and a good dress. Kate and Maggie thought she was somewhat boring, but they never challenged her after she once threatened to whip them. They had a sixth sense she could be inspired to harsh punishment if not treated with the utmost respect. The rising table incident also gave them pause regarding what other powers she may have. Moreover, she was fearless about snakes. Once, a snake came into the yard and the girls watched it swallow two live baby chicks. They ran and told Baba who immediately grabbed a sharpened shovel and chopped the snake in two. The two chicks came running out from its belly unharmed.

Baba and Ginger claimed they loved the "Nigras," as they called them and they did not like Abraham Lincoln. "The worst thing that ever happened to the South," Baba muttered stubbornly, when Kate came home from school extolling the accomplishments of the great president. "Cousin Jeff Davis should have been President of the North *and* the South." She was as solid as a rock on this matter. Parke and Ginger often fought during discussions about the Civil War, but he lost when Baba came to stay because now it was two against one. It would be a long time before Kate fully understood the brand of "love" her mother's family felt for the Black people of the South. The prejudice was so deeply embedded they would never so much as catch a glimpse of it.

Baba completed the sewing circle established by Ginger and Clara Bell. They would busy themselves with ordering fabric through the mail, making patterns, sewing for the whole family, knitting, and embroidering. Fabric could be ordered using order sheets torn from ladies' magazines where fabric textures, colors, and available prints were displayed. After the patterns were made, the fabric yardage required careful calculation. They ordered cotton for the girl's dresses and underwear, sheer cotton voile for good dresses for the women, silk for slips to wear underneath, and lawn for bed linens. When the packages arrived, they dropped everything to engage in a sewing marathon that often lasted late into the night.

When the gardening season was over, Ginger and Baba canned all the vegetables from the garden. When they ran out of these, they made catsup and spaghetti sauce with the last of the tomatoes and hung the remaining herbs from the rafters to dry. These industrious habits not only set them up well for the winter but also kept Ginger from dwelling on her worries.

In 1937, Indian summer was giving everyone a false sense of security with its sunny, mild days that lasted into November. It was even hard to get in the holiday mood without snow. However, Ginger and Baba stayed up late sewing and knitting presents for Christmas. Parke was out on his quarterly sales trip through Illinois. This usually took him about a week, if all went well.

On Saturday afternoon, Mimi took Kate, Maggie, and their cousins to see Shirley Temple in *Heidi*. Cousin Bob was "in love" with Shirley Temple. He had a framed picture of her on the stand by his bed. Halfway through the movie, the girls were crying so much that they had to leave the theater. Mimi took them across the street to Kresge's dime store to buy big daddy-sized handkerchiefs. Then, with composure restored, they returned, armed to see the rest of the movie.

Later that week, suddenly, the temperature plunged to twenty-seven degrees. Ginger got up at 3:00 a.m. to turn on Leo the Lion. The temperature in the house had fallen to fifty-two degrees. They already had all the blankets from the chests and closets on the beds. Maggie woke up crying. She had wet the bed and was freezing cold, so Ginger helped her change and brought her into her bed to keep warm. The wind was whistling through the old house, the shutters rattled, and Jack Frost painted patterns on the windows.

The next day remained heavily overcast, the wind died down, the thermometer held at thirty-two degrees. Everybody in the house started fighting. Ginger got mad at Baba because she let the kettle boil dry, melting the bottom out. Kate blew up at Maggie and knocked down her house made of blocks. Old Leo purred away, blowing hot dry air up through the registers, but the house still felt cold. Ginger made vegetable soup for supper, let one of the barn cats in that was crying at the door, and they all went to bed early. Just before falling asleep, Kate heard the cat growling as he toyed with a mouse who had also come in out of the cold.

In the morning, a light snow flurry was scudding about the yard. Ginger drove Kate and Maggie to Pleasant Valley School, a redbrick, two-room structure up the road. One room was for first through third grades and the other was for fourth through sixth grades. Though Kate was only nine years old, she had been moved to the room with the older children as she quickly absorbed the lessons. Kate kept her snow pants on all day because her desk was not close to the wood stove. All the kids' attention stayed on the excitement of the first snow of the winter. They were busy looking out the window instead of paying attention to the teacher. From where she sat, Kate could see into the other classroom, where the two children who always hid under the teacher's desk were even peeping out to see the snow. Their elderly adoptive parents had denied them schooling until the truant officers dragged them in at the age of seven. They had never had contact with the outside world and, so far, they had not said one word.

The snow flurries built up speed and by noon the flakes were sticking to the ground. Everybody stayed inside and ate their peanut butter sandwiches and bananas at their desks. Kate had brought a thermos of hot soup and felt guilty eating it. Just after lunch, the teacher decided to close early. The teachers and janitor drove children home who lived too far away to walk. The snow had covered the grass and gravel by the time Kate and Maggie trudged up the drive so they slipped, slid, and scrambled up to the house. Little did they know this would be the last breath of fresh air they would get for some time.

By dusk, the family could not see the barn through the heavy falling snow. Quietly, peacefully, they became enveloped in the snow's arms, cradled snugly in the little house listening to the comforting purr of Leo and the crackling static of the popular radio programs: "Jack Armstrong, the All-American Boy," "Captainnnn Midnight," "Little Orphan Annie," who gave clues to use on decoder rings, which they had sent for, and "The Lone Ranger." Maggie was in love with the Lone Ranger and kissed her pillow effigy of him to Kate's immense irritation. Then, a newscaster was warning about a blizzard. Too late; you could look outside the window to see that.

Baba made a Jefferson Davis Pie for after dinner. Such a rich, unconscionable dessert! She brought the recipe with her from Mississippi, which was mostly butter, brown sugar, eggs, cream, dates, raisins, and pecans topped with fluffy merengue. Sickening and devastatingly delicious.

By morning, there was a two-foot blanket of snow cover. The sun came out briefly, but by noon the wind picked up again, blowing snow against the windows, while tree branches scratched the glass trying to get in. As dark approached, the howling gales of maniacally laughing winds threatened to corrupt everyone's spirits as the tentacles of wintry blasts tightened their grip. Their small circle of heat diminished to an isolated spark and became lost in the vast universe of black snow.

Morning came late because the daylight could not get through the windows. The house remained in darkness and they all slept in. When Ginger turned on the light, she saw the clock read 8:40. She checked the thermostat: sixty degrees. She turned it up and went to look out the front door. When she pulled it open, a wall of snow faced her. Only one window on the opposite side of the house allowed for a narrow glimpse at the top of the outer world. From there, she could see the road—that is, the place where the road used to be. Now it resembled the rolling dunes of a desert. Tree branches bowed, nearly touching the ground under the weight of the snow. Others lay broken on the fresh sheet of white crystals.

It will be days before we are out, she thought. *Oh, my God, I hope we have enough oil in the furnace tank and food!*

There was no way to check the oil gauge on the tank in the cellar, the only entrance to which was the slanting door outside, now covered in six feet of snow.

Thank God, the electricity is still on. It's a wonder. It could go out anytime!

She began to envision breaking up furniture to burn for warmth. Her thoughts racing, she realized that the electric range was their only way to cook, now regretting ever replacing the old cast-iron kitchen wood stove. She madly pulled everything from the refrigerator that could go into a stew, opened canned vegetables and beef broth, filling two large pots hoping to get it cooked and, at the same time, adding extra heat to the house to hedge against an outage. It worked. Within three hours, the stew was cooked and Baba had baked cornbread and biscuits. They were set! It was a good thing, because around 11:30 a.m., the lights went out. They lit a kerosene lantern. Maggie and Kate played with their Patsy Ann dolls and Baba and Ginger tried to sew by the dim light.

When night came, the girls were both complaining of headaches and they fell asleep right after supper. "They probably have headaches due to the lack of fresh air in here," Ginger told Baba.

By morning, the house was quite cold. Baba told the girls to stay in bed while the two of them dressed in odd assortments of clothes to keep warm. Parke's tweed suit pants with turned up cuffs and suspenders, topped with his jackets over their sweaters, made them look like clowns, but they were warm enough.

Once they were dressed, they turned their attention to the kids and discovered both were running fevers of 102. As the women nibbled on cold biscuits for breakfast, the girls fasted until the fevers broke. "Feed a cold, starve a fever," Baba intoned. Buck, much to his embarrassment, made a mess on the floor because he could not get outside.

Late in the afternoon, they heard a muffled commotion. After a while, the kitchen door burst open and there stood Will Zantow, breathing hard, icicles on his nose, and frost on his eyebrows. He could hardly stand. He had been shoveling for nine hours today and six the day before to get from his house next door to theirs, a matter of about 800 feet.

After he rested a while and had a good laugh at the clown suits, he went back to his house and soon returned with a pot of hot soup and an apple pie. Mrs. Zantow had stayed overnight, unwilling to travel back to town when the snow began and had cooked on Will's kerosene stove. The girls were starting to feel better and Ginger let them sip soup with a piece of pie. Ginger thought of Parke and had a passing wave of resentment that he was not home with them, while having a drink with Will and playing Hi Low Jack.

Maggie recovered from the fever quickly, but Kate remained down with a tight chest. Ginger tried to call Dr. Johnson, but the phone lines had broken from the heavy snow. Baba proclaimed she needed a mustard plaster. She prepared a paste of dry mustard, flour, and water, spread it on a piece of sheeting, slapped it on Kate's chest, covered it with flannel, and stood back. "There. Now get well."

Mimi would have said "beef tea."

Baba brought a piece of string to play Cat's Cradle with her and when Kate finally asked for some Franco-American spaghetti, they knew it was over.

When the snow melted down to rolling hills rather than peaks and valleys and the temperature rose to forty degrees, Ginger and Baba allowed the girls to go out and play. Ginger stuffed them into bulky snow pants, galoshes, hats, mittens, and scarves and they headed for the pasture slope with the sled. Ginger sent Buck along as a baby sitter. He half rode the sled and half tumbled down the hill; then, with the rope around his neck, he pulled the sled back up. When the light began to fade, he tugged on their mittens, trying to make them go home. They were so tired of climbing through the deep snow that they fell, panting and laughing, and wet their pants. When the warm wetness turned cold, they mustered the strength to get to the house, where Ginger and Baba pulled off the soggy snowsuits and made hot chocolate for the girls.

Letters from a
Silver Hill

HARRY DIED IN 1938 and they buried him in the Daven-port cemetery on a blustery, cold winter day with family, friends, and employees in attendance. He had been noticeably ill and losing weight for months, but the family did not speak of it. Their Christian Science beliefs were all that they needed to accept God's ways as gracefully as possible. Mimi hosted an open house memorial service and many business associates traveled from afar to pay their respects. H.C. Lusk & Sons continued under Allen's financial leadership and began to recover, but not before almost all of Harry's savings were exhausted to weather the toughest years of the Depression. Keeping employees, most of which were relatives, had been Harry's main concern, even when it meant lowering wages. Now, things were getting better.

By this time, Parke was able, once again, to pay full dues for his family to enjoy the benefits of the club. As the girls grew taller, Parke introduced them to horseback riding there. This played directly into their horse fantasies so it was an easy sell. They squeezed the price of lessons out of their budget and, when they could not afford it, Parke conducted his own coaching. Maggie quickly got disillusioned. After a few good falls in front of her school peers, she started finding excuses to skip lessons. She, like her mother, preferred the social nature of the club environment. Kate, however, was a natural. She learned fast, quickly shook off disappointments in the riding ring, and excelled. Ginger supported her by sewing her fashionable riding outfits. Parke and Kate grew close riding trails for hours.

Kate was eleven the next year and left the small rural school to attend Saint Catherine's Episcopal school in Davenport, where her parents hoped she would be more challenged. She had completed all the lessons Pleasant Valley School had to offer. Parke drove her each morning and they talked about her studies and dreams for the future. Kate excelled at Saint Catherine's and her best friend, Alice, was the other high achiever in her class. After school, Kate and Alice took the inter-urban streetcar to the country club for riding lessons, trail rides, and just to sit and do homework and talk. They were happiest in their riding jodhpurs and barn clothes.

One afternoon, as they lounged on bales in the hay barn, Alice asked Kate how many children she wanted to have when she grew up and got married.

"Who says I'm getting married?" shot back Kate. "It's not required is it?"

"Well... no," replied Alice, "but what would you do instead?"

"I want to be a book writer. I could do that and still have a husband, but having kids seems like a big distraction."

"If you get married, your husband will expect you to have his children," Alice insisted. "And, if you don't get married, you will be lonely. And how would you support yourself?"

"I told you. Book writer. Famous author," Kate quipped.

"You are silly. I bet you change your mind as soon as some handsome man asks for your hand. I want at least four kids. I'll have a big brood of children to love and spoil. Besides, they can take care of me when I am old and decrepit," Alice mused.

They both were quiet for a minute, imagining themselves as old women.

"It's all pretty hard to imagine us being old like that," Kate replied. "Let's make a pact to be back here dancing at the club when we are ninety years old."

Alice laughed. "Okay, it's a deal."

Parke picked Kate up at the club at the end of the day. He admired his oldest child and could make her feel like the most important person on earth with only a look, squeeze, or well-timed silly joke in soothing contrast to the jealousy Kate felt about her mother's close relationship with Maggie. Kate worked hard to please Parke and he, in turn, worked hard to make her feel loved.

On weekends, the whole family was at the club. Parke would play golf or ride with Kate, while Ginger and Maggie sat on the wide porch overlooking the greens, having refreshments, visiting with friends, playing cards, and reading the newspaper and magazines. They liked discussing the latest fashions and marveled at news from afar.

M EANWHILE, IT WAS OUT of sheer loneliness and bore-
dom that Mimi began methodically going through
everything in her enormous house. Agnes helped her sort
through clothes, family mementos of earlier days, and papers
in Harry's study where she discovered letters addressed to him
that began arriving in 1929. Harry had never discussed the
mystifying letters with her and their meaning was confusing.
Sensing their importance, she gave them to Parke as her eldest
son.

The first was handwritten in large bold letters.

Tegucigalpa Honduras, C.A.
May 28, 1929
Mr. Harry C. Lusk Davenport, Iowa
My Dear Kinsman:
I am writing to inform you and all your mother's living chil-
dren on my appointment as Curator in the estate of Major E.A.
Burke, deceased. I have some names and need addresses if you can
provide them. I have one, Roy Anson Lusk, (No. 238, Front Street,
New York City). What is your relationship to Henrietta Lusk?
A cable message was sent to American Consul Shaw, here, from
Florence Lusk-Weiblen of South Milwaukie, Wisconsin. I wrote
her at length a few days ago, enclosing a copy of my Curator's
Report, and requested further information regarding kinship to
Major Burke, etc. Who is she?
I would appreciate a full statement from you, supported by your
affidavit, covering fully the feature of relationship to the Major
of all of your Lusk and Parke families—including, of course, your
aunt, Mrs. Susan Olds, now deceased, and her descendants.

I desire such statement for my files regarding all such members of said families who may consider themselves heirs-at-law of Major Burke within the effect of the laws of Honduras.

I send you, enclosed with this letter, a copy of my Report No. One. The information is <u>strictly confidential</u>, and I request that you send this on to your family in New York City since supplies of same are almost exhausted. Ask them each to <u>write</u> me <u>here</u>, at No. 14 Calle Concordia, stating that they have seen the report. Some of the kin are too poor to advance me any money—a fact which renders it essentially necessary that those who <u>are</u> able to shall come quickly to my financial relief.

As to my standing, I refer you to any U.S. Senator or Congressman from Texas, my home state. My present home is Breckenridge. See, also, Who's Who. Please write me fully and promptly.

Sincerely yours,

Wm. C. Hawkins, Curator

This, and others, were among his papers, evidently set aside to be dealt with at a later time. It seems there had been some follow up, but the paper trail mysteriously stopped without resolution. Could it have been because of the devastating market? Or maybe Harry's health began to fail—perhaps as a result of the worrisome business problems that began a few years later. Or something may have happened to Hawkins.

Mimi put Parke in possession of the papers ten years after they were written. He was reading them aloud to Ginger. The first letter from Honduras mentioned some names of aunts and uncles Parke had heard flung about in casual family conversation, but he had never heard of Major Burke. The Curator who wrote the letter said to check Who's Who for his name, Wm. C. Hawkins. Parke went to the library and found no such name. The Curator's Report No. One revealed some details about Major Edward Austin Burke's death, his property, and last will and codicil.

Parke lit a cigarette and continued reading to Ginger.

CURATOR'S REPORT NUMBER ONE

Major Edward Austin Burke, a citizen of the U.S. of America, died on Sept. 23, 1928, in his room in a hotel in Tegucigalpa, the capital of the Republic of Honduras, in Central America. His age was eighty-seven (87) years. For about forty years he had resided in Honduras.

President M. Paz Baraona, who was his personal friend, sent a military guard of honor, and proclaimed a period of national mourning for his distinguished friend and benefactor of Honduras.

Upon request of the municipality of Yuscarán, Major Burke's body was interred there.

"Who is this Burke, anyway?" asked Ginger looking up from her latest therapy—a rag rug.

"Damned if I know," Parke uttered through a cloud of smoke. "Your dad ever mention him?"

Parke shook his head, reading on to himself, then aloud:

...believed to be the most extensive and valuable gold and silver producing properties under one control anywhere in the world. They include an extensive group of mines at Yuscarán and

vast governmental concessions, embracing both placer and quartz mining properties, in and along and between the Guayape and Jalán rivers. I hold proof that these properties are of very great value.

THE LAST WILL AND CODICIL OF E.A. BURKE

Major Burke left a will, made in 1896, and also a codicil to it, made in 1899, in compliance with Honduran laws.

Between the execution of the will and the codicil, Major Burke's only son, Lindsay Gaines Burke, an officer in the service of King Leopold of Belgium, was killed in action, in the Congo, in Africa, and his death induced the execution of the codicil.

One half of the estate was to go to his wife and the other half to his son. Since they are both gone, I am the sole survivor of the four designated in the will. He was my mother's brother. The American Consul at Tegucigalpa and the local court have designated me as the Curator of the open estate.

By the terms of said codicil of 1899 the usufruct...

"What does that mean? Usufruct, sounds obscene," ventured Ginger as she pulled up a red scrap of wool.

Parke closed his eyes and searched his memories from law school. "It means the right to utilize and enjoy the profits and advantages of something belonging to another."

"Oh, well, there you have it. Not worth a thing." He read on:

But this only applies to a certain portion of Major Burke's Honduran estate and is to be applied to the establishing and maintenance of schools for manual arts, industries, and mines, for the benefit of the young men and women of Honduras.

Under the settled laws of Honduras, as declared by the Court of
Appeals in a noted case. Such usufruct is not a proprietary interest
in the corpus of the property itself, but is merely beneficial interest,
and consequently carries no right to the possession of the property.

The late slanting sunrays reflected off some dancing dust
motes and odors of something savory undulating seductively
from the kitchen. Though Parke had not known the degra-
dation of standing in the bread lines, he had witnessed great
change. Income had diminished, and Handsome Harry's fortune alone had kept the family business going until the savings
were gone.

A certain gloom like brown moths fluttered in the darkened
corners of the room outside the cold glow of the lamp as Parke
tried to concentrate. *This information from a world unknown*
seemed unreal and, yet, here I am, he mused, *and here is this*
strange material in my hands tingling in its enticement.

Ginger returned with a fresh highball and he continued to
scan the letter and summarize the points to her.

"Since the provisions of his will were never executed because
both his wife and son had already died, it was as if Burke had
died with no will at all. So, by law, the estate passes to his next of
kin and heirs-at-law. Now comes stuff about the last will of Mrs.
Susan Elizabeth Burke, his wife, who died in 1916, naming her
granddaughter, now Mrs. Linda Montgomery Jeffrey. Evidently, she had a child by a previous marriage. Some of the property
acquisitions were after 1916. This could be important."

He went on, "Then there's a thing about an outstanding
mining contract made in 1927 with an American contrac-

tor concerning exploitation, development, and sale of certain quartz and placer mines and mining properties near Yuscarán and the Olancho District. Some $800,000.00 in gold was due in installments. The contractor defaulted."

Parke read what Hawkins had to say about this:

Since my qualification, on Dec. 1 as Curator, I have devoted practically all of my time and energies to this far-flung and somewhat complicated estate. Manana is the bane of all Latin-American countries, and estate proceedings, especially, involve many exasperating delays.

Parke took a long drag on his Chesterfield and heaved a sigh. "Well, it goes on but those are the high points. It's hard to know what to make of it."

Parke and Ginger put the documents aside and said no more about the matter, but Parke found himself thinking about it at odd times. He wondered if something could come of it. Would it be worth pursuing? He had questions. Perhaps he should consult one of his lawyer friends, though his budget hardly warranted hiring legal counsel. What did it mean if he was an owner of property in Honduras?

Honduras? Where exactly was that? What could one do with this mining business, short of borrowing large sums of money to operate the mines? Money. That is probably the reason the contract in the Curator's Report was not completed.

Parke continued pouring over the possibilities in his mind. The contract dated January 31, 1927 was less than two years before the stock market crashed in October 1929. The banks failed in 1932 and 1933, and final suspension of the gold standard marked the trough. In 1933, there were more than twelve million people unemployed in the United States. It was highly probable that this was the reason the contract had not been satisfied. The American had very likely suffered a financial setback when the market crashed. In 1929, when the Curator first wrote to his kin, Harry Lusk's food broker-age business was doing okay but required all his attention. H.C. Lusk & Sons had done very well during the 1920s.

Now, looking over the dates and the Report, Parke saw that Burke was buried at Yuscarán. He found a map of Honduras at the library and located the town and the rivers of Jalán and Guayape. He began to have fantasies of explor-ing the jungles of Honduras and rescuing his family from mediocrity with a new business venture.

Parke found himself going over the papers many times, often in the middle of the night as Ginger slept. He found a genealogy with the papers. William Hawkins was Major Burke's nephew. Burke was Parke's grandmother's broth-er—his great uncle. Parke, then, was a third cousin to Major Burke. All the first and second cousins were dead. Another "confidential letter" from Tegucigalpa dated June 26, pro-vided more details of the Burke properties.

CONFIDENTIAL
June 26, 1929
Memo No. A.

Since the date of my Curator's Report, I have devoted much time to study of the Burke concessions in and along and between the Guayape river and Jalan river and it seems:

That the original Guayape concession and Guayapa extension cover about 120 miles to within 70 kilometers of the confluence with the Jalán and 500 varas on each side of the middle of the streams.

Altogether these total concessions embrace about 715 square miles of mineral territory and include several mines of demonstrated value.

Some of said concessions, approved by the Congress of the Republic of Honduras, carry <u>perpetual</u> exemption from all taxes, present or prospective, and exemption from more onerous provisions of future mining laws, all such exemptions constitute <u>rested rights</u> which are protected by the constitution and laws of that Republic and by the existing treaty between that Republic and by the United States of America.

All of said concessions are separate and apart from the Burke gold and silver mines (some 24 in number) at Yuscarán.

This letter rambled on regarding Hawkins' desire for power-of-attorney, which would require letters from all heirs stating such. He suggested perhaps selling the properties or forming a corporation and issuance of capital stock for shares distributed among all claimants.

The astounding fact that these very long hand-written letters were sent to *all* claimants (some eleven or so in total) and that Hawkins was so adamant and enthusiastic made the situation sound desperate. Dated three days later, another dispatch provided more details.

June 29, 1929

My Dear Cousin:

Your letter of 14 June reached me today and I thank you for it, and for your desire and efforts to provide for my financial assistance in the way of advancement. Probably it is difficult for you to comprehend how badly it is needed. From time to time, it actually gets down to a question of sheer subsistence and stationery and postage, rendering the sending of even small sums of money timely and of grave importance in enabling me to stay on the ground and hold down a difficult and complex and very serious situation. I need sources of abundant funds for carrying out my general plans for the estate.

I did not have money for having the "Memo No. A" typed and do not write on a machine, so I request that you return it to me here for my files.

My correspondence on estate matters is very heavy. I mailed out 13 pieces yesterday, and today's mail brought me 14 pieces.

From the list of heirs that you sent me, I have contacted all the 11 second cousins who are next of kin. Most cannot or will not advance any money for estate preservation. They have sent affidavits of heirship, but Charles A. Olds of Albany, Ill., writes that he is an old man and cares little for wealth in any form.

Correspondingly, they ought to be willing to sell their shares at low prices if I can find people who are willing to make such speculation.

Certainly, it was very kind of your brother, Roy, to invite you and your wife to accompany him to Honduras, but the trip should not be postponed until fall. Then you can see things as they are and help me over the crisis in the strenuous fight to save the properties from the hands of the spoilers.

If they manage to drive me out of the country, they will thereby permit administration to pass into the hands of their representatives.

I have news of the death of B.F. Brightman, one of the Burke kindred, and the death of 4 in an automobile accident in Texas, and of the very serious sickness of still another in Texas.

Those of us who are spared to carry on ought to be drawn closer in this great cause.

Sincerely yours,

Hawkins

Harry had corresponded with Hawkins, giving encouragement and sending money. Matters were proceeding with a list of heirs and elimination of some. The next letter, dated about a month later, becomes more personal. Hawkins was feeling more optimistic and the hope of absolving some of his difficulty appeared imminent, or so it would seem.

July 31, 1929

Dear Cousin Harry:

Your kind expressions of confidence on the part of yourself and other members of your family is greatly appreciated. I assure you, I am making every effort to protect and conserve, with fidelity and zeal, to the fullest extent of my capabilities.

I am having a hard struggle to find means of subsistence and the necessary stationery, postage, etc. I am holding on, grimly, keeping the boat headed upstream, and hoping for early relief. So far I have only received $383 from the Confidential Report.

Since I wrote you in June, I was down for 4 or 5 days with a fever. I took medicine, including 90 grains of quinine, and am back at work. Recently, I have given careful attention to several different matters in the courts and have plans to meet with the President regarding the usufruct and the undivided interests of Mrs. Jeffrey.

I have been patient and persistent in the face of many perplexities, and now it seems evident that Mrs. Jeffrey, the mining contractor, their joint agent and attorney, and the government have come to the conclusion that the Curator is to be reckoned with in all matters relating to the Burke properties.

Said contractor's over-due installments to said estate now amount to about one quarter of a million dollars, in gold.

I note your suggestion that the E.A. Burke heirs should give me power-of-attorney, and it may be necessary for me to use that in order to deal promptly with orders as may lie within the jurisdiction and authority of the local court wherein said estate is being administered. The situation may be presented any day.

We look forward, hopefully and eagerly, to your visit. Send me, as soon as possible, a radiogram indicating when you will reach Puerto Cortes from New Orleans.

Hawkins

And, so, it was left. It made sense to Parke, given the timing of the national economic crisis. Harry was undoubtedly very worried about a venture that could have endless needs for capital at a time when there was none. The matter remained unsettled. Tegucigalpa, meaning "hills of silver," in the exotic country of Honduras, and Yuscarán, meaning "place of the house of flowers" in Nahuatl, the language of the Aztecs. It was so irresistibly intriguing. He could not ignore it and it ate away at him causing distraction and sleepless nights.

He went over and over scenarios in his head where he might go there to find out more. Then he thought it would be selfish to leave Ginger and the girls alone. But what if it could change their lives? Then, he remembered how these third-world tropical countries were rife with disease and political unrest. Was it even safe to go there? His wheels spun and spun trying to get traction on a course to follow.

Parke longed to talk to his father and find out what he really thought of the prospects. Harry was pragmatic and very astute at business. He also had years of experience dealing with all types of people. *How did Harry know whom to trust?* Parke trusted everyone. It was just his nature to be empathetic and kind. Sometimes, when Parke was out on sales calls, he would find himself daydreaming about what he and Ginger now called the Silver Hill Letters. Deep in thought, he would end up taking wrong turns, missing road signs, or becoming lost in the countryside. This made him arrive home late making Ginger worry more than usual. He felt bad when this happened, so when it did, he would stop at a roadside stand to bring her home flowers.

Deep Waters

IT WAS ON THE sixty-eighth hole of the weekend when Parke walked up to the tee box and cracked a brand-new Spalding smack into sparkling Duck Creek and found himself barely able to maintain a demeanor befitting a gentleman. He almost cursed. The impulse to throw his clubs into the water after the ball was practically uncontrollable. On a Sunday afternoon, with only five more holes to go, suddenly his game fell apart. His par, birdie, eagle roll began to look as if it would end in a bogey, double bogey horror show. It was the end of summer, which he had spent every spare moment on the golf course, and he was getting worse rather than better. Overhead, V after V of geese honked on their journey south. The cool, fall days whispered a hoary forecast.

Parke dug a Titleist out of his pocket, in case it would make a difference, retained his poker face, and sliced it into the edge of the woods. He was a lefty and usually a noteworthy contender, but he felt himself slipping lately. The trek around the course took a toll on his leg that had recently become a constant reminder of his horse accident during the war. His hair was thinning and the sun burned his scalp, so he took his handkerchief and tied a knot at each corner to make a hat. It served the purpose, but his partner who always wore a snappy straw hat in the fashion of Sam Snead made fun of it.

Seeing the migrating birds swept his thoughts toward the south with them and bright visions of silver and gold dimmed the sight of the fickle-figured golf ball. She, with her seductive beckoning, so elusive, so alluring, so heart rending. To hell with this love of my life, he thought, meaning golf. The lure of the Silver Hill Letters tugged at that place in his soul that had never quite been completely satisfied.

He pulled a five iron from his bag to chop out of the deep rough for a nice plop onto the green, missed a twenty-foot putt by three feet, and sank the three-footer for a double bogey. He had watched the three others in his foursome make a par, a birdie, and another par. After a long drink of iron-laced water from the tin cup at the pump, he shanked the next drive and landed in the wrong fairway.

By this time, Parke was half-way to New Orleans, the land of Dixie Jazz, in his mind. They were now on the final hole of the weekend. Even the much-anticipated nineteenth hole was losing its appeal. That is when he knew.

In the years after Harry passed, things had turned brighter and the food brokerage business was improving. It was now 1939; ten years after Curator Hawkins had begun the desperate effort to save the Burke estate. Parke was regaining financial confidence and the lure of the tropics was beckoning. It meant leaving Pleasant Valley for a spell, but he felt the enticing mystery of the estate papers too much to brush under the rug. He left the club to go talk things over with Ginger.

Ah, fool. It's a mid-life crisis. Forty-four years old he was, of course! Ginger knew it. She was only thirty, but she realized his sudden inability on the golf course could not be brushed aside. They talked until 4:00 in the morning about the obsession he was developing toward Honduras. She half-heartedly tried to sway him but saw it was useless. It would "only be for a few weeks" he said and Ginger was intrigued enough herself to eventually encourage him.

She listened and understood, and even worked hard to convince him that she could manage quite well in his absence. After all, she already did everything that was required for the family's daily subsistence. She did not need him for that. She needed him for financial security and emotional fulfillment. He had arranged for the bare necessities money-wise and she declared her ability to put emotional requirements on hold. At that time, Ginger did not know that her crisis would come later and last much longer with devastating consequences. For now, she was the strong one.

They agreed he would book passage after the holidays, but as soon as the decision was made, he wanted to leave immediately. He showed the girls the books and maps from the library so they would understand where he was going. Kate, now eleven, asked Ginger what exactly he was going there for. She was no longer satisfied being treated as a child. Ginger said he had business there, which made zero sense to Kate. She knew what her father did for a living.

"Is he going there to source new products for the company?" Kate asked.

"Maybe," Ginger told her. It just seemed better for the girls not to know too much. There was a lot at stake and it was private family business, not something about which to spread the word. Allen was the only other one who had seriously looked over the papers. He thought it was an expensive lark and that Parke should focus on the business and his family. Given their history, Parke was not about to take any advice from his younger brother. Allen always seemed to have his own agenda and they never felt a true closeness.

There had been one last letter from William C. Hawkins.

Puerto Cortes Honduras, C.A.
September 3, 1939
Mr. Parke H. Lusk Pleasant Valley, Iowa
Dear Mr. Lusk:
Word has come to me that your father passed away last year. My deepest sympathies are extended to you and your family. Your father was very supportive of my efforts to resolve the Burke estate and sent me some money to relieve the dire straits of my financial position.

Since 1929, I have tried to accomplish a settlement, but mañana never comes. They talk about proceedings, but the results are elusive. At times I have almost given up hope, but my original commitment as Curator has kept me tied to it.

As you see, I have moved to Puerto Cortes, living now at No. 9 Calle
Oscuridad. There has also been some time during which I could not stay with my work because of recurring setbacks with malaria.

By now, the heirs-at-law have mostly become third cousins of Major Burke. Please contact me regarding your claim to this estate.

Sincerely,

Wm. C. Hawkins

A cablegram to Hawkins announced Parke's intention of paying him a visit. When Hawkins received it, he damned near went into a panic. There he was, stewing around in the steaming tropical quagmire of his enclosed patio. It was the rainy season and it had been pouring for seventeen straight days. The place was breathless and squiggling with chameleons and skinks, oozing with mold and mildew, and writhing with choking parasite strangler figs. Land crabs grabbed his legs in the dark and clamored at the jalousie doors. Arm-blackening mosquito hordes threatening to devour him.

When the rain would cease for a day or two, and perhaps the full moon would rise above the canopy, Honduras' treasury of the finest mahogany would yield one perfect tree from 1,200 acres. Men felled it by the light of the moon, amidst the screaming howler monkeys and squawks of brightly-plumed parrots, toucans, and macaws. Below, the stalking jaguars and ocelots would move invisibly through the palmettos while anteaters routed in the underbrush and the fearsome *fer-du-lance* would slither into a rift of a rosewood tree. Parke would soon be entering this exotic world, but the flora and fauna were not nearly as strange as the circumstances.

W.C. Hawkins' gaunt appearance, his cadaverous sunken eyes, his Abe Lincolnesque silhouette, most certainly intensified by bouts of malaria, all presented a problem toward presenting a creditable façade. It was going to be difficult to explain to Parke Lusk all that had happened in the last ten years. Still, Parke's interest in the matter had rekindled a spark of hope in Hawkins for financial help. Little did he know Parke was on a treasure hunt himself, with big dreams but scant cash.

In mid-October 1939, Parke bid his wife, children, and mother-in-law farewell with lots of hugs and kisses and instructions not to worry. They were to stay safe and focus on everyday life. He promised to write often and return as quickly as possible. He took the train to New Orleans, spent a night there in a seedy hotel near the docks, and the next day boarded a passenger vessel sailing for Honduras. The voyage took two days of navigating farther and farther south into warm waters and humid air.

The steamer docked at Puerto Cortes to unload its cargo and a few travelers on October 20. The Curator recognized Parke by his height, mainly, since he was not the only arrival from the States who wore a white linen suit. It was a trending fashion of the 1930s among international travelers.

A short time earlier, William E. Hawkins, the nephew and Curator of Major Burke's estate, had put on his other white shirt, the one without a frayed collar, and tried to smooth the wrinkles in his black serge suit. He had sponged off spots on the lapels, tied a gray-striped tie tightly at his throat, and taken a deep breath on reflection of his appearance. Now, looking at the tall American on the landing, he realized this meeting was of critical importance to him not only for financial reasons but also for his self-esteem. He had begun to lose faith in his ability to perform the duties for which he was trained. In Texas, he was a lawyer and an important member of the business community. But in this country the laws were different or non-existent. Business for him became extremely frustrating since every procedure that required astute decision-making was put off until *mañana*; everything was always *mañana*.

From the docks, Hawkins and Parke picked their way over cobblestones and the body of a drunk, down several crooked, narrow cart paths littered with dog excrement and garbage, past walls with doors—some elaborately carved—which hid courtyards from sight. The walled passageways yielded little insight into the lives of those inhabiting these quarters. Parke felt a certain astonishment at the secretive and unyielding silence of this labyrinth. They turned corners at crossroads only to move down another alleyway. The same; always the same. He felt he could never find his way out of this crammed hive. After walking about a quarter of an hour, Hawkins stopped at one of the doors in a wall. This one was uncarved, plain and weather worn, and as gray as driftwood. He reached for a bell beside the door and, after giving it a jostle, put his ear to the door listening for approaching footsteps. Hawkins' wife, Maria, eventually opened the door and they entered a small courtyard. A few containers of pale pink and white geraniums, and a wall covered with orange bougainvillea, were the only ornamentation. A table was set for three under a balcony with two glasses, a bottle of tequila, sliced limes, and a small glass dish of salt.

Hawkins' wife, a plain, thin, dark-complexed woman, prepared a meager meal in celebration of Parke's arrival. A pot of beans simmered on the woodstove. She had learned to make corn tortillas and there was soup of chicken broth with tomatoes and hot chilies. Special for the occasion was a flan for dessert. The last coins from the weekly food budget went for a bottle of *aguardiente*.

After dinner, Hawkins poured tequila for Parke and himself and ventured a hesitant suggestion that they visit the magistrate's office to seek a sanctioned visit of the mining properties. "That is, if you are willing to make the rough trip." It was exactly that for which Parke had hoped.

"This place will get to you, like it has me. It has many hidden treasures, of the past and for the future. You will see." His eyes blazed with excitement. On the other hand, it may have been the fever coming back.

Parke stretched his long legs out in front of him, leaned back and lit a Camel. "I had an interesting conversation with the captain of the ship. After we had crossed the Gulf of Mexico and were steaming down along the coast of Yucatan, he told me about the Gulf of Honduras, which was named by Spanish explorers. He explained that Honduras means deep waters or profound depth of intellect, feeling, or meaning. It means abstruse, ambiguous, and mysterious. Fascinating!"

The tequila was beginning to wield its stealthy influence. Parke could feel the grasp of the tropics toying with his mind. Tree frogs tuned up their instruments for a symphony depicting the story of ancient Mayan rituals of bloody sacrifice to the gods. The sound was hesitant—distant at first. Then, it grew as their ventriloquism threw voices into the surrounding jungle. A throbbing rhythm pervaded through the very thin walls and their music increased in volume as more frogs joined in to reach a mind-smashing crescendo.

What was Hawkins talking about now? Parke refocused: possibilities of wealth, and many untapped mineral deposits of silver and gold. Opportunity for investment. Parke asked Hawkins how he had made ends meet for ten years in this foreign country. Hawkins explained he survived on simple legal work for Americans living in Honduras.

That night, Parke slept on a narrow *palate* in the back storage room of Hawkins home. The heat and humidity made it difficult to sleep. He missed Ginger and the girls and wondered what he had done coming here. *Was Hawkins reliable?* How could he solve issues that Hawkins could not solve after ten years of trying? He finally turned off his thoughts and found some restless sleep in the wee hours of the morning.

M EANWHILE, BACK IN PLEASANT Valley, Ginger was cutting out a cardboard profile of a large-sized person. "I'm going to stand it up in the window with the light behind it at night, so anyone passing by will think they see a man in the house. It's my protection plan," she told Mrs. Zantow. Ginger laughed a little at herself.

Mrs. Zantow looked sternly disapproving. "You know, I tank you crazy letting your husband go off like dat." She sent Will over to the house with a gun. Will was shy and nervous, and starting to develop an inappropriate crush on Ginger. He tried to show her how to shoot, but his hand shook so badly that the gun went off at the wrong time, sending a bullet into the chicken house. A great raucous occurred as setting hens flew the coop—feathers flying and chickens cackling. Ginger decided it would be better if she taught herself to shoot. She never did, but once when Parke's cousin Brent stumbled into the house in the dark of night, she almost shot him. He was only drunk and looking for a place to sleep it off before his wife, Charlene, would let him in their house.

Then she received her first letter from Honduras.

October 18, 1939

Dearest Ginny,

This old freighter seems to stand still in these calm seas. I can't see any land, but we must be moving at a snail's pace. Twenty knots per hour, they said. The only thing of interest is watching the porpoise play in the waves of the bow and the flying fish soar above the top of the water. At night I make wishes on the falling stars which shower the black velvet skies.

I'm anxious to get to Puerto Cortes and meet this Hawkins in person. Hope I'm doing the right thing. I guess I would never have been satisfied if I didn't at least try. Who knows what's ahead?

I hope all is well with you and the dearies. And Baba, too. My thoughts are always with you, but I hope (I know) you understand. Who knows? Maybe we'll get rich!

Tonight for supper we had beans (again). I'll be glad to get back home for some steak and French fries. What say?

There is a queer iridescence to the crest of the waves. Tell the dearies I think it's fairy dust.

By the time you get this letter perhaps I'll be deep in the interior of Honduras. Whoops, I forgot my pith helmet. Cheer up! Be home soon, Love.

P.

Ginger received this letter three weeks after Parke wrote it. She was already feeling the effects of stress. Her bravado appeared in good order on the outside, but inside the tension was building, her tectonic plates were slipping, and the earth shook under her feet. Will had an infected foot and Ginger went to "doctor" it. He wanted her to do it instead of his mother. Besides, Ginger would have a drink with him and play gin rummy.

In the last days of October, a night came when Buck did not come in to eat dinner. Kate found him in the barn laying in the straw. He refused any food or water for three days despite her efforts to entice him. Ginger asked Will to come put him out of his misery. Kate lay in bed with her fingers in her ears not wanting to hear the gunshot. She heard it anyway. Will loaded Buck's body into the wheelbarrow and took him to the stand of trees at the bottom of the ravine where he dug a grave and buried him.

The girls and women cried that night and went to bed early. Kate and Maggie missed school the next day since their eyes had nearly swollen shut from crying. Kate could not control her weeping and missed a second day of school after that. Finally, Ginger said, "Okay now, Kate. That is enough. Buck lived a good long life for his breed. We could not save him. You need to go to his grave and say your final goodbyes and get on with living."

Kate went and sat on a rock next to Buck's grave. She went over in her mind the day Parke brought him home when they all exclaimed that, for a puppy, he was the size of a full-grown dog already. Then, he just kept getting bigger. Kate, Maggie, and Buck were a threesome. He watched over them and protected them, worrying when they were sick, and giving them big sloppy kisses when least expected. It was a horrible rite of passage to lose a beloved friend like this. But she knew well enough that nothing, including all her tears, could have saved him from the fate of his short canine life on earth. At last, she stood and said aloud, "I will never, ever forget you."

Screaming
Jaguars

HAWKINS PURCHASED TICKETS TO take the train to San Pedro Sula the next day. Parke was traveling light with one small suitcase. He was not equipped for camping, which could become a necessity, so a hammock was required, some emergency rations, and raingear had to be bought. Although October promised drier weather, it still was raining every afternoon. Besides his dress suit, he packed some riding breeches and boots left over from his days in the cavalry. It was his hope they could acquire horses for the journey. Little did he know how hard that would be.

Parke was anxious to be on the move. Time was precious and he hated the tropical coast. Climbing to the interior would bring cooler temperatures and fewer mosquitos. The first night in Puerto Cortes proved to be miserable. Mosquito netting hardly helped. The bugs had a Bacchanalian feast.

The train consisted of an engine, a tender, a combined baggage and freight car, and a passenger coach like a streetcar with seats running lengthwise. The trip was only thirty-eight miles, but it took all day because of stopping every three or four miles to deliver goods brought from the docks and to pick up and let off passengers with their sometimes-surprising packages, such as baby pigs in a mesh shoulder bag, goats on leashes, and chickens in boxes.

As they approached San Pedro, the hills rose to the south. The city was beautiful with tree-lined streets covered with riotously blossoming vines. The International Hotel provided them with the last decent dinner and bed accommodations they would have for some time. The well-appointed dining room had mahogany furniture and the menu, though limited, included some enticing items to choose from. Parke ordered chicken cooked in banana leaves served with a large salad accompanied by some fruits and vegetables that Parke could not identify. His room had fine window screens, as well as mosquito netting, that together allowed for a good night's sleep. In the morning, a servant tapped on the door and delivered a washbasin and a jug of warm water.

Locals advised them to go by wagon to Lago de Yojoa. Hiring a *mozo*, or guide, who could help them with interpreting, finding *posadas*, and managing their luggage would not be expensive. The wagon and *mozo* were to show up at the hotel at 5:00 a.m. This highly recommended *mozo*, named Jesus, arrived at 7:30. Parke and Hawkins sat in the dining room, where they could watch for Jesus, drinking enough *café con leche* to keep them awake for the next three days. Hawkins took the opportunity to begin his story.

"I have been here now for ten years. My law practice and connections back in Breckenridge have suffered. My health has been damaged and there are those who have said I've lost my sanity, but I assure you that is not so. In the beginning, my enthusiasm gave me the momentum to keep up with all the correspondence and court proceedings, but as time wore on with few resolutions my strength waned. It was more frustrations and setbacks than my illness, I believe. There were times when I was in a fever, yet managed to attend meetings with Mrs. Jeffrey's lawyer."

"How did all that turn out? Did she get her share?" Parke asked.

"It's been settled. But the deal with the mining contractor is not. Oh, you don't know what I've been through. And my poor wife. All this time away from her family. In this land."

"Why did you move to Puerto Cortes?"

"It was to be closer to a means of escape. The *caudillos* politics is sometimes difficult. Now, with the new President, Don Tiburcio, he is powerful! Just to look at him! He is six-feet, six-inches tall, barrel chested and with piercing eyes and a flaring *mustachios*. When Baraona was in office, it was peaceful and I felt that he was my friend since he was close to Burke." Hawkins seemed to drift off in thought. "They were afraid I was a political dissident."

"Were you?" asked Parke, squinting against a blue smoke screen.

"I was not totally happy but they didn't need to throw me in jail. I was in that stinking place for five months. God! What a hellhole. I still don't know what happened to allow my release. Usually, they have a way of dismissing you from their minds when they slam the doors. Perhaps they needed more room for worse villains than me."

About that time, a figure, all in white, emerged from the morning fog, like an apparition, leading a skinny, dark mule pulling a rickety wagon with one bench seat and a buckboard. The *mozo* wore a broad-brimmed pith hat, leather thong sandals, a machete, a pistol, and a gourd. He smiled broadly and made no excuses or apologies for being late. They quickly threw their equipage on the back of the wagon. Jesus jumped on the seat and took the reins. Parke climbed up beside him, leaving Hawkins to ride on the buckboard, legs outstretched, facing backwards, with the cargo.

They rattled slowly out of town with mixed feelings of anticipation and dread. The early road was good and fairly level running beneath groves of coconut palms that shaded them from the blazing sun. They passed through village settlements of adobe huts with red tile or thatched roofs. The road deteriorated the further they progressed and their pace slowed considerably. Parke was hoping that after they crossed Lago de Yojoa, they could find horses to make better time. Already, they had regrets about the present mode of travel. Walking would be faster, especially when they climbed out of the valley and the road became little more than a trail.

The first night was approaching. The afternoon rains came and they proceeded huddled under their rubber ponchos. A welcoming light from a shelter was elusive. After several more miles along the road, a glimmer appeared on a hillside. Jesus leapt from the seat to scramble up the rocky slope to a small adobe house. Parke and Hawkins followed. A broad woman filled the doorway. "*Dos reales,*" she demanded, then brought tortillas and coffee. They hung their hammocks in the shed over the stove and roosting chickens. The hammock was better than sleeping on the ground but not entirely comfortable.

That night, Parke dreamed of yellow eyes piercing the jungle wall like flashlights. Tied to a tree, he could not move, but he felt serene in spite of the wild jaguar's hungry eyes. He woke with a start when a piercing scream shattered the night.

The next morning found the woman of the house awake before dawn. She brought boiled eggs and ripe bananas. She asked if they had heard the haunting shriek, then told the story. Hawkins translated for Parke.

"It is the angry Moon Jaguar searching for his princess. There is an ancient Mayan temple nearby where a king named Eighteen Rabbits died. His son, Moon Jaguar, was sacrificed to accompany the nobleman into the next world. This young prince had fallen in love with a princess and he promised he would return for her. Ever since his bloody death, the Jaguar's frightful screams can be heard as he searches for her through the jungle night."

When the purple night turned to green, they were already creaking down the road again. Jesus was a taciturn fellow, not given to conversation. Therefore, Parke amused himself straining his eyes searching the surroundings for exotic species and trying to adjust to the culture shock. He saw a magnificent oscillated turkey, much more brightly-feathered than those in Iowa. Other bright parrots and macaws festooned the trees making their squawking presence known. They passed small settlements of no more than a few huts, all with garden patches, and an occasional colorfully skirted woman standing by the road, never going anywhere.

They reached La Guama by evening, a village on the shore of Lago de Yojoa near the ancient pyramid sites of La Ceiba and Los Naranjos, a vague pile of rocks, now poking their grizzled heads above an emerald patchwork quilt. That night, they spent in a barren, dirt-floored room with two other travelers waiting to ferry by small steamer to Pito Solo. The woman of the *prosada* provided a halfway decent meal, which included some strange meat. Armadillo, they said. Parke thought they were likely toying with him.

Sam Smythe, an English cockney gold prospector, was the captain of the midget steamboat, which he built himself. Parke met him after dinner.

"I came here in 1914 to escape the war—thought I'd get rich panning gold. Married this Mayan woman, Lago Azul, who gave me so many *niños*, I had to expand my horizons, so I built this boat to carry travelers across the lake. It keeps me in beer."

Parke enjoyed a room-temperature mug of draft with Smythe as he approached the question of horses on the other side of the lake.

"*Es possible, Señor.* I know a man in Pito Solo... if he is not dead drunk. Most travelers go by motorcar these days, taking the long way on the passable roads, or they go by mule over the mountain. Horses are rare, though I heard this man had won a horse, gambling. He does not know what to do with it. They say the animal is too rank."

Next morning, as the sun crept over the hills, a terrible clacking came from the lake and a thin plume of smoke reached through the morning mist. Two piercing toots announced departure time as the five passengers straggled along the reedy path to the tiny boat, which looked like it would barely hold all of them.

Soon, the heavy mist burned off to reveal spectacular scenery in all directions. Jade-green water, purple mountains, and clear powder-blue skies decorated with whipped cream clouds helped Parke to forget the jungle cat dreams and once more imagine gold and silver. The fifteen-mile trip passed quickly and they soon docked in Pito Solo. After securing his boat, Smythe and Parke went looking for the man with the horse. They found him at the edge of town, snoring in a hammock, which Smythe spilled on the ground sending pigs and chickens flying. *"El gringo quiera caballos. Arriba!"*

Smythe steered him to the cantina, where, after a couple of shots of *aguardiente*, the man became coherent. He could get two mules and a horse, but the *gringo* would have to buy the horse for the exorbitant price of twenty-five *lempiras*. Parke gave him eighteen.

The "wild" horse stood, head hanging, in a muddy corral with two long-eared mules. The mare was flea bitten, gray, skinny, and slightly goose-rumped. Parke slid back the gate bar and sidled cautiously into the enclosure. The animals studiously ignored him. He spoke softly to them and eased toward the mare who had now turned her head to stare with large black eyes at the approaching man. She presented her rear end to him as a warning, it would seem. The watching Smythe and smirking Mestizo expected the mare to kick. Parke whispered to her, reaching out a hand to scratch her rump. She backed up, shifting her weight from one foot to the other, enjoying herself. The audience gaped in disbelief.

Parke worked his way slowly up her side, making small circles with his fingertips to emulate the nuzzling lips of horses. He patted the soft flesh of her chest and ran his fingers gently down the sides of her face, under the eyes, and finally smoothed her ears. Then he turned and walked away. She followed him.

"That horse will kill you," stated the drunk.

"We will see. Hand me the bridle." Parke easily slipped the bit in her mouth and led her out of the paddock. What he did next astounded the growing onlookers. He simply lay over her back, eased one leg over her rump to sit astride, and rode off down the road at a brisk walk.

The horse came with an old McClelland saddle with outrageous brass shoe-like pointed stirrups from the Spanish Conquistador era. Parke felt like Don Quixote. His comrade, Hawkins, mounted a mule and Jesus loaded the other one with cargo, which he would lead. Parke bid farewell to Smythe. And so, they were off to tilt windmills.

That evening in camp, Parke's thoughts drifted to Ginger and he wrote:

October 25, 1939

Dear Ginger Baby,

Well, we're on our way. The first few days were almost overwhelming. So many new sights and sounds! It's been exciting and we've been lucky. No Mishaps. Our spirits are high. The best part was a beautiful trip across a pristine lake. The surrounding mountains spoke of a mysterious history, legends, superstitions, and alluring prospects.

We're following a road, of sorts, which goes to the capital. Though I saw one touring car go by, it was traveling slowly because the way is covered with rocks. There are mostly ox carts. I think we're better off on horseback. Oh, yes, I bought a horse. She's a spirited little mare of Arabian stock, who everyone said was unmanageable. They simply didn't understand her. They had beaten her and tried to break her by throwing a heavy bronco-busting saddle on her and making her buck. She learned too fast for them. All they did was teach her to buck. Now she is fine and travels way out in front of the others, never tiring, and always eager to see what's around the next corner.

The land is very hilly, always up and down. Some beautiful flowering trees, and large fern-like trees. The aguacates are in bloom attracting many kinds of hummingbirds that fight and dive at our heads.

We should reach Comayagua tomorrow. It is the old capital city and should provide us with a comfortable place to rest.

Love to you and the Dearies,

P.

The next day, they bought bean *burritos* with *salsa fresca* from the hotel to eat along the road for lunch. It was uncomfortably warm and humid and sometimes difficult to stay awake. Parke's thoughts drifted aimlessly through imagined conversations with the authorities about regaining control of the properties. He saw himself winning favor and getting things settled where Hawkins had not. He dug deep to find the right voice and confident air to practice winning the day.

Capital Gains

T HE PROMISE OF CAMAYAGUA loomed enticingly before them. Parke's indomitable spirit finally cracked. "When I get to the old capital I'm going to head straight for the bar. After I've had enough drink to stop the pain in my butt, I'll have a hot shower, eat a civilized dinner and hit the sack. They do have real beds, don't they?

Hawkins responded with a shrug. "The beds are slightly better than a hammock, but the showers may surprise you."

After passing through towns called Palmerola, Flores, and then Tamara, they approached the great city. The bustling Camayagua did, indeed, seem like a very welcome respite after roughing it along the way. The gleaming white of the palace and churches promised a measure of culture in this heathen land. They rode across a long bridge approaching the city and a couple of large touring Cadillacs, passed by. The Hotel Casagrande had a spacious, barren room with three beds of thin mattresses without springs on boards. But it was clean with large windows opening out on the street.

Soon after they checked in, Hawkins disappeared into the city. Parke went to the hotel bar and Jesus took care of the animals and equipage. The dark little saloon was empty at 3:00 p.m. except for one light-skinned man brooding at a round table in the corner. His face was sunburned and roughly whiskered and beneath his broad brimmed hat, bloodshot, glittering black eyes penetrated the gloom. A half-empty bottle on the table told of the man's immediate goal: to drown.

"Dakota's the name, or Dak if you're a friend," he muttered and nodded an invitation for Parke to join him. Silently they drank and smoked together bound by some common unnamed thread. "What's your game?"

Parke could not quite warm up to this stranger. "Passing through."

"To where?"

"Yuscarán."

"Ah, place of the house of flowers. I've been there, and everywhere else in this land for that matter. Fifteen years. Looking for gold. Panning mostly. All the good concessions are tied up. The best, besides Rosario, is in the hands of a Major Burke of New Orleans. He organized the Honduras Gold Placer Mining Company in 1889 to work in Olancho. The working capital then was $250,000.00... a lot of money in those days. A lot now, for that matter." Dak took a drag of his cigarette before continuing.

"As far as I know, they never did hit the mother lode. They planned to turn the River Jalán at Retire, south of Juticalpa, in order to work its bed. The Major also had the Guayape and Jalán Companies."

Parke said nothing.

"Are you interested in prospecting? What did you say your name was?"

Parke swallowed and felt uneasy. He decided this stranger did not need to know his business. He declared his name was "Tex."

"So, you're from Texas?"

"Yes... well actually NO," he blurted out, afraid he would have to talk about Texas, of which he knew little, except for the few months he spent in the Army boot camp. Actually, I'm from Iowa."

"Iowa—where the tall corn grows." Dak's interest waned.

Parke's interest, on the other hand, became intense after hearing this man speak of the very thing for which he had come. He poured them another drink, hoping not to seem too eager, asked, "Do you know where this Major Burke is now?"

"Last I heard he was in Yuscarán, but then he spent a lot of time in Teguci, too. He used to be quite a friend of the good President Baraona."

Ah, then he does not know of his death, mused Parke. *Could be he has been off in the mountains too long.*

"Tex, this place will break your heart. If you can escape the typhoid and malaria. If you can be lucky enough not be bitten by the *tamagas* or confronted by a mountain lion, you can languish beneath the magnificent blue of the sky. The splendor of the tropical sunshine, the brilliance of the myriad stars, and pine-fragrant breezes rushing through the mountain passes will seduce you, but in the end the loneliness and nothing but toil from morn' 'til night—no break—it will crush your heart. Many men have lost their fortunes, minds, and hope in Honduras. I could have been better off to spend my inheritance on one of these old houses. In the past, during the turbulent years, residents buried their treasures under their homes before fleeing from invaders. Others have dug until the house collapses, to no avail."

"How do you happen to know so much about Burke?" Parke asked.

"This is a very small country—made even smaller by the limited number of *gringos*, who talk of many things over the demon rum. Little goes unnoticed."

"Then why didn't you notice that Burke died seven years ago?"

There was a long pause as Dak raised his eyebrows and stared into his drink.

"I've been in Mosquitia for seven years. Only returned to civilization recently. Still have some catching up to do I guess."

"What goes on in Mosquitia?"

"I was led there by curiosity. Wild men—Aborigines! There are strange customs there. Long ago, when missionaries tried to convert them, they introduced ideas for celebration from England like the maypole dance. Maypole finally became something quite different than the missionary's concept of gay spring rite dances of children around the beribboned pole."

Dakota appeared slightly deranged as he rambled on. His eyes were rolling about and a grimace flashed across his face at times.

"It has been outlawed, but they do it anyway. It starts after dark under a big tree in the forest. A pole, ritually erected to represent the phallus, is part of an ancient Druid custom. Drums beat out a hypnotic rhythm, the people gather, and one especially-adept couple dances together in the firelight. Their movements explicitly depict the act of copulation. It is pure sex. One cannot watch without becoming aroused. Soon, other couples join and the fever goes on into the night. Gradually couples move discreetly off into the forest. The fire dies down and the moon comes up. It's the tribe's way of insuring the perpetuation of their race."

"Sounds very much like what happens in the good ol' U.S.A. every Saturday night."

Dak swung his head around and stared at Parke. "Yes, but there's a veneer of gentility at least."

"A very thin one. Easy to see through. It might be refreshing to experience a more honest ritual." Parke, who actually thrived on polite society's flattery and flirtations, surprised himself with that remark and felt a bit embarrassed.

"Please excuse me," Parke said as he stood, preparing to depart for the anticipated luxury of a hot shower.

About that time, the sounds of gunshot blasted the quiet streets. People started running, some only in their robes. He could only believe that an insurrection was occurring and felt he must seek shelter. Bang! Bang! It was coming from all sides—even from the very bowels of the building.

Dak laughed loudly at Parke's consternation. "They didn't tell you? It is the showers. The plumbing is only on from four to six. You want a shower. Now's the time. Ha."

When Parke entered their hotel room, Hawkins had materialized. "What happened to you?" asked Parke.

"Looking for a *farmacia*. The old malady plaguing me again. Need a little rest. Be okay tomorrow."

After a satisfying hot shower, Parke wandered down the street and found a vendor operating out of a thatched-roof shack selling fresh hot *tamales* wrapped in banana leaves and filled with spicy chicken. He bought a bottle of beer to go with them and sat on a small stool under the awning of the modest business. It was delicious and set him up for a dreamless, solid night's sleep.

The next day, Hawkins was better. His fever subsided and he was able to share a breakfast of *huevos rancheros* and strong hot coffee with Parke. They prepared to travel on.

Jesus was already at the stables preparing the animals to move on. For once, the horses received good feed rations and Parke's mare was especially feisty. By the time they rallied and prepared to ride out, she pranced around, tugging at the bit, eager to see the world.

They were nearing their goal to make it to Yuscarán, where Parke hoped to bring this odyssey to fulfillment, or at least find some answers. In the beginning, his quest was a matter of curiosity, like a genealogical study to discover himself. Somehow, he felt that if he identified this portion of his heritage, it would lead to a way to alleviate some of the longing torturous turmoil in his soul.

The "land of the house of flowers" was said to be a magic kingdom where a large church presided over a den where a golden dragon lived. Could this actually be the mother lode known by the ancient Mayas and protected by the sacred place of worship? The church was always filled with the flowers that grew so profusely in the surrounding countryside.

Yuscarán was said to be an active mining town with an interesting social structure, including cocktail parties, bridge games, and genteel ladies from cultured parts of Europe. Many enter-prising men from Europe and the United States had invested in this new frontier at the turn of the century. The place had un-doubtedly settled down some since then, but Parke envisioned there would still be an infrastructure and an air of civilization.

According to the map, the distance to Yuscarán appeared short enough to cover in a couple of days, but it failed to show the verticals. They could set their sights on a distant steeple, but then suddenly come upon a precipice overlooking a deep *barranca* into which—by way of narrow, twisting, switchback trails—they must descend a thousand or more feet to the river at the bottom, passing from misty cloud forests to rocky, piney woods and hostile cactus land.

The animals pushed through the river and it was a trick to keep the equipage dry. At one deep stream, Jesus carried the trunks on his head. He had longer legs than the mule.

In October, it was nearing the end of the rainy season, which began in May, bringing luxuriant growth, riotous red and yel-low flowers, emerald valleys, and sapphire and azure mountains. Tree ferns, exquisite orchids, and wonderful delicate maiden hair ferns abounded.

Parke found himself floating in a dreamlike realm, rocking along on his rhythmic gaited mare, watching her twitching ears listening to him, and then eagerly looking forward to the next turn in the road. She loved to travel and explore the ever-chang-ing terrain; as happy to clamber up the steepest paths as to canter the soft-shaded roads of the lowlands. To Parke it felt as if they were making good time, but Hawkins on his mule lagged behind. The *mozo*, on foot and tending the pack mule, trailed even farther behind. It gave Parke time to stop, occasionally, to take mental note of the astounding abundance of strange plant life. Once, he found himself in a forest of nasty-tempered capuchin monkeys, who threw sticks and tried to urinate on him from the trees above. Sometimes, his horse had to step over *lianas* hanging in loops to a foot above the ground. Parke's imagination saw himself swinging like Tarzan from the *liana* ropes, whooping his wild animal call, from tree to tree with the monkeys.

Some stretches up and down the mountains had steps like marble and he heard waterfalls singing in the distance and birds talking of love to each other, enthusiastically claiming their territories. An exquisite honey-gold voice of a *jilguero* bewitched him. He or she was unseen yet all around him. He brought the mare to a stop and quietly dismounted. The song emitted from nearby, sometimes in front of him, sometimes in back, but the singer mysteriously remained hidden. Then, suddenly, there it was, only two yards away: a tiny gray bird on a low branch. It was the most beautiful bird-song he had ever heard. Its ethereal quality portrayed the strange spirit of these green cathedrals. The little enchanter beckoned deeper and higher into the realm of enormous trees rising one-hundred-and-fifty-feet toward the heavens, all festooned with hanging, swaying mosses and covered with weird parasite and epiphyte species never imagined in Iowa.

Iowa. The thought shocked Parke, who was not only thousands of miles away from there but eons away in spirit. *My God! How could I forget?* It frightened him. What power this enchanted forest had over him! He suddenly imagined the great *lianas* entwining him in a death grip, like the snakes in Lao-coön's struggle for life.

When Hawkins came clacking up the rocky path, his long legs scraping the ground, he did not look well. He joined Parke in a welcome respite from the saddle, sinking to a downed tree with an elaborate sigh. As he did so, he barely missed squashing a large black lizard.

"I've traveled this route before, but this time it seems to be longer," said Hawkins. "I remember once I was coming from Yuscarán, carrying some gold nuggets that I panned from the Choluteca. A couple of *banditos* waved some huge old pistols at me and made off with my little treasure. That is one of the biggest problems here—not *banditos*—but the lack of good travel routes or any means of transporting products. Back in the 1860s, the United States loaned Honduras twenty-five million dollars to build a railroad across the entire country. They only built about fifty miles. Seems the money went into the hands of politicians and foreign promoters of the banana industry. All the gold and silver that had been mined had to go out by mule-back and accompanied by heavily armed guards. Maybe that's one reason for the lack of extensive exploitation of some of the still buried treasures of this country."

That brought Parke back to the business at hand. "Let's be off," he urged. They were plodding down the mountain once again.

Since it was raining every afternoon, they decided it wise to set up camp in the early afternoon and build some palm-thatch shelters over their hammocks. The next day started before the night was done.

The cathedrals they had seen at the old capital city started Hawkins on religion. "They claim Catholicism as theirs but it's all mixed up with Indian superstitions in some places. Up in these hills, there are many little secret pagan shrines built of piled-up pottery shards; sometimes you'll see a crudely-carved image of a god or saint and candles burning. Some are in caves, while others are on open hillsides. Festivals spring up at the drop of a hat. It is an excuse to stop work, dress up, and get drunk. The Waiknas, an Indian tribe, worship the devil they call *mafia*. Most believe they must worship to seek good luck and protection from the ever-present forces of evil. Among them are designated sorcerers, who act as directors of conscience, fortunetellers, and physicians. The "physicians" have little bags of quartz crystals and beans they use in solitaire games to decide a patient's fate. To determine if the sorcerer's medicine will work, they play the game three times. If the doctor gets encouraging vibes, he continues the treatment. If the game decides "no," then there is no further attempt to heal. The people abandon the ill-fated victim to die. No food, no water, no medicine."

Hawkins rambled on. "There is one place around here where they believe that St. John and the Virgin Mary had a love affair on the night of the crucifixion. To prevent a repetition of this event, their images are locked-up on Good Friday in separate cells of the local hoosegow. The next morning, their respective confraternities come and, for a couple hundred pesos a piece, bail them out."

Hawkins' complexion was taking on a yellowish tinge. A fever smell formed an aura about him. "Or was that in Momostenango?" he muttered. "Well, at any rate, as Aldous Huxley so aptly put it, many people in Central America are staunchly heathen and devoutly Catholic."

Yuscarán was their goal, but they only made it to El Zamorano.

A certain fierceness was trying to break out of Parke's outer façade. Maybe the shell would crack. *Stay calm*, he said to himself. *This is only the beginning.*

Doubts started to creep in. Why was he here? What was the goal? Was it just avarice, plain and simple? No, he merely desired financial security for his family. Painful pictures of tiny, red-chapped hands, cold, wet feet, fevered convulsions, and weeks of failing business endeavors flashed across the movie screen in his head. Desperation had driven him to the extreme. Like a fool, he figured if he went to Honduras the prospects would greet him with open arms and all the grand possibilities would become clear. Instinctively, he would know exactly what to do. Like he always said, "It's fun to make money." He still felt that exuberance of youth with its inalienable belief in unlimited possibilities.

That evening, lying in a hammock in a room with the whole peasant family of a small *posada* along the road, Parke pulled out his pen and notepad to draw a skinny bones cartoon by the light of the dying fire. Then he wrote:

October 30, 1939
Dear Ginger,
As I lay here in my hammock, the rain pours down, even after it stops raining, because the foliage is so heavy it drips for hours after. I'm dreaming of you. As I ride along, all the wondrous landscape

becomes imprinted on my brain and I mentally practice describing it to you. It would be easier if you were here to see for yourself.

It's strange how in the high selva we see little wildlife. Maybe it's because the creatures are so easily hidden in the lush growth. And then our horses moving through the woods probably scare them off. I did see some monkeys and some bright, noisy parrots, macaws, and toucans. There was an enchanting birdsong that I believe could have the power to lure me into trouble. It must be the most beautifully-haunting music in the world.

Oh, yes, last night there was an arresting sound in the distance. A strange, sad, musical note descending the scale. OO-oo-oo-oo, rather like a pipe organ with a stirring human quality. It came closer and closer and then moved away again. The voice, was quite eerie, lovely, and distressing. Our guide Jesus said it was a giant anteater, an óso caballo.

He shot an animal for our supper. It looked kind of like a big rat but was quite tasty. Paca was its name. A nice change from corn and frijoles.

Keep the home fires burning... if you know what I mean.

P.

They rode on in the morning. The creaking of the saddle, the mare's flowing mane, and the odd, uncharacteristic chattering of Hawkins made the time pass like melting snow.

At high noon, under a blazing sun, they entered the sleeping city. The place was almost a ghost town. It had flourished during the height of the mining industry, but now it was no more than a deserted village with decaying buildings and rock-cluttered roads. Gone were the days when mule trains—each consisting of fifty mules carrying loads of silver, gold, and quartz—came through on their way to the southern port of San Lorenzo. Now, a single church stood in the quiet streets, faithfully ringing its bell every hour, day and night.

Agreeable people politely offered assistance regarding a *posada* and stabling facilities. In no time, they were ensconced in private rooms. Indian maids brought jugs of warm water for bathing. They were told they were expected as guests for dinner at the Fortin House.

That evening, after a very fine meal of roast pork and cool wine, Parke ventured to ask their host, Francoise Fortin, if he knew the location of Major Burke's grave.

Monsieur Fortin, with an expression of raised-brow surprise offered, "But of course, in the *jardin* across from the church. There is a statue, of sorts. Why do you ask?"

"He was a relative of mine... a third cousin."

"Ah. And you want to pay your respects?"

"In a way. Actually, I'm interested in his mining properties... from an historical viewpoint, that is."

"Hmm. Well, there might be more information at Tegucigalpa. I do not know. I believe his concessions were widely spread. His connections were thick with the president... all of them. He ran in the top circles."

Parke enjoyed a pleasant and very welcome respite from the rigors of travel over the most delicious cup of coffee ever, brewed from beans grown on the nearby mountain.

Throughout the evening, Hawkins had been remarkably silent. Parke thought he was intentionally taciturn in hopes of surreptitiously learning something new from Fortin. Had he looked closer, he would have recognized that feverish flint returning to those deep-set eyes and a languid appetite for dinner.

By morning, Hawkins could not get out of bed. He did not show up for breakfast and Parke found him shivering under his blankets in his room, his complexion jaundiced. They sent for a doctor who pronounced his malaria had returned. "He shows signs of severe anemia and the fever is persistent."

"But only yesterday he was well," Parke insisted.

"I will need to examine some blood smears under the microscope to be positive, but there still only remains the *cinchona* bark... and the grace of God... for a cure. We must try to keep the fever down to avoid brain damage."

The mestizo servant was engaged to apply cool compresses to his head until the fever broke while Parke left to explore the "house of flowers."

Damn this Hawkins! he thought. He had counted on him helping to achieve any possibilities of progress. The man seemed to be losing his mind, which greatly worried Parke. He was no longer the person who wrote those letters with such optimistic enthusiasm. *Perhaps it is all too damn late*, he wondered.

The main street leading up to the church was lined with pink *mimosa* trees and alternating blue *jacarandas*. The utterly astounding beauty should have been enough to lift Parke's spirits, but he was in a dark mood. He picked his way over the cobblestones with his head down in deep thought. Rising in gleaming splendor like a mountain of marble, the church stood guard over its golden dragon.

MAJOR EDWARD AUSTIN BURKE

1841 – 1928
UN CABELLERO BRAVO Y SIMPATICO

Parke passed his hand over the words in an effort to commune with his cousin's spirit. In effect, it was like a silent prayer—a contemplative seeking for guidance. Was he beating his head against a wall of stone?

Parke wandered the streets and surrounding countryside all day until he found himself at a mining site located in the hills. There, he experienced the awesome raping of the beautiful land; the monstrous ripping apart of the precious earth to pick out some relatively tiny vein of gold or silver to be used in man's eternal quest for material wealth and political power. Before him lay a great scathing, devastating scene, infested with workers moving like parasites. He was shocked. It caused an explosion in the center of his body, as that of seeing a child fall from his bike and skin his beautiful face. There were giant machines, scurrying men, big holes, axes, picks, clanging, shouting, and huge eruptions as "*Cuidado!* Fire in the hole!" warned of another dynamite blast.

It was becoming apparent to him that the whole, vast enterprise involving numerous mining operations required a plethora of specialists: mineralogists, explosive experts, machinery mechanics, and supervisors—not to mention hundreds of laborers. However did Burke manage? All his connections were now unconnected. *Maybe one could lease out the properties and take a cut of the profits yielded*, mused Parke.

He suddenly recalled that he came from a long line of risk-taking entrepreneurs. Parke began to doubt his stomach for such fortitude.

Meanwhile, Hawkins' condition worsened. His fever remained too high for too long. His pulse was racing and then weakened. Attempts to administer the quinine resulted in vomiting. For three days, the man clung to the edge of the abyss of death. Parke stayed nearby. The fourth morning, as Venus stealthily rose in the east, perversely rotating in the wrong direction, William E. Hawkins breathed his last death rattle and escaped into peace.

Parke sent word to Hawkins' wife and arranged to have his body transported back to Puerto Cortes, a gruesome affair given the lack of embalming fluid. Now, Parke was on his own. He prepared to backtrack north to Tegucigalpa, where he hoped to talk with the president. Naivety about how to go about this would turn out to be on his side.

Chameleon

A FTER ANOTHER LONG DAY trekking on horseback, they arrived at Tegucigalpa in the shadow of Mount Picacho. This time the *mozo*, Jesus, rode Hawkins' mule and his name became 'Sus, for short. Their relationship became more companionable.

After they checked into the hotel, Parke dug out his linen suit and sent it for cleaning and pressing for his appearance at the presidential palace. His plan was to announce himself, present a letter of introduction from a lawyer in Davenport, Iowa, and hope he found Mr. President in a receptive mood.

While Hawkins was with him, this bold move would have not been wise, because of his presumed enemy status. Now, the situation was different. Parke could slip into his own chameleonic style.

The next day, rested and ready, Parke left his hotel on foot for a bracing walk to the palace to find the main gate heavily guarded. Eventually, a small, uniformed, unhappy man came out to speak in Spanish to the guards, who liked to rattle their sabers menacingly. After an hour's wait, the gate opened and then closed loudly behind Parke.

The United Fruit Company, whose strong financial power overwhelmed Honduras like a great octopus, backed the
president, Don Tiburcio Carias Andino. He represented the
National Party and, through sheer indifference by the Liberal
party, he won office in 1932. M. Paz Baraona, a gentle doctor
and Liberal Party candidate agreed to assume the presidency
temporarily in 1925 to please the United States who had asked
to intervene in their internal affairs. By *continuismo*, he retained
that position beyond the legal terms of office. He really had no
taste for high-powered politics, preferring to live the life of a
bon vivant and excelling in great personal charm suited more to
diplomacy.

Therefore, when Don Tiburcio took charge through strong
caudillo political methods he received no opposition. The National Party newspaper, *La
Epoca*, bombarded the public and Honduras willingly knuckled
under. He was economically unsophisticated, politically con-
servative, and a strongman ruler. His very physical appearance
demanded respect.

This was whom Parke prepared to meet. He had with him a
copy of the Last Will and Codicil of E.A. Burke and wished to
inquire as to its validity at this time. At first, Parke had paced
back and forth, smoking several cigarettes, but then gradually
changed his color to adjust to the upcoming scene. He saw himself cooler and suavely in control. He envisioned his own dis-
arming smile charming the man and he believed the encounter
would be easy and smooth.

After a long wait in a massive hallway, the little man returned
to wave him past more guards. He led Parke down a long,

echoing hallway. Double doors swung open at the far end and Parke saw the man, enveloped in blue smoke, standing at a sunlit window. As he approached, the man turned to greet him, but he was not smiling. Hawkins' earlier description of him was spot on, right down to his penetrating eyes. "I have seen your letter of introduction. What do you want with my time?"

"Don Tiburcio, Mr. President, I am most pleased to meet you. I have traveled far for this honor," announced Parke, flashing his best smile.

The president softened a little and half-smiled, despite himself. "What brings you to this country?"

"I would like to show you some papers I have regarding some mining concessions."

"Mining? Why don't you go to the Department of Mines?" the president barked, showing impatience.

"Because, you, sir, are in charge of this country and it is you who can tell me what I need to know."

Well, of course, Don Tiburcio was quite flattered at hearing this. The fact was he really did not know much about mining... not that his pride would allow him to admit it. He stuck out his uniformed chest, raised his chin, and glared at Parke.

Parke took that as a cue to go on with his petition. "If the good president would allow me, I have these papers. It will only take a few moments of your precious time."

"Yes, please make it quick. I'm a busy man." In truth, he did not have any plans for the rest of the day, but it would wreck his image to say so.

Parke presented the papers to Don Tiburcio with underlined passages:

... perpetual exemption from all taxes, present or prospective, and exemption from more onerous provisions of future mining laws, all such exemptions constitute rested rights which are protected by the constitution and laws of that Republic and by the existing treaty between that Republic and by the United States of America.

"Ha, my good man, this was written a long time ago. We have a *new* constitution. It is all different now. I am in charge. These papers are worthless!" The president casually tossed them across the desk.

If Parke had been less naïve as to the political system and its dictatorship, he would never have ventured into the presidential palace. Now, all he wanted to do was leave. It was apparent that this man had no interest whatsoever in Parke or his papers. For a long moment, he faced Don Tiburcio. It was difficult to know how to react. There was an expression of abject consternation on his face, even though he felt as if he was in control. Utter dismay came over him. He had not expected such crass behavior from the country's leader. Somehow, he expected him to be intelligently reasonable and have deference for a foreign visitor who had traveled so far. Parke was confused. He felt heat rise in his face. He did not know whether it was anger, embarrassment, or fear. His experience did not prepare him for a situation of this kind. The palms of his hands suddenly were sticky and he heard his own heartbeat throbbing in his ears. It occurred to him that possibly Tiburcio did not know what he was talking about. Perhaps his reaction was merely that: a temperamental explosion derived from ignorance and arrogance. He was so overly convinced of his own importance, that Parke's audacity had allowed him no other choice.

Now, realizing there was nothing more to discuss, Parke wanted to get the hell out of there. But how? The man did not dismiss him, seeming to derive pleasure from the situation. It occurred to Parke that he could possibly change the subject and divert the anger.

"This is my first visit to your country," he started. "It is quite beautiful. You must be very proud." Flattery always worked for Parke. It was a mainstay of his social graces. It never failed.

"And, if I may say so, your palace is magnificent." Personally, he thought it appeared to lack miserably in furnishing, far too sparse and barren for the opulent tastes of North America and Europe.

Tiburcio responded as Parke had hoped. He began pacing back and forth in front of the big window, surreptitiously glancing down into the courtyard. Finally, he smiled, offered his hand, and moved to usher Parke out.

Parke felt foolishly exonerated. The day was a total loss except that he found out about the new constitution. Some loss of hope; some gain of knowledge.

He returned to his hotel and lay on the bed staring at the ceiling until dusk. Waves of anxiety passed through him as he contemplated what to do next. He thought of his family and how he should write a letter, but he had nothing to say. Eventually, he slipped into a restless slumber and dreamed he was working as a laborer in that horrible pit he had seen a few days earlier. The clang of machinery, axes hitting rock, and foremen barking orders and obscenities rang in his ears. He awoke feeling horribly homesick.

After finding breakfast of eggs and sausages wrapped in warm flour *tortillas*, he sat down to devise a plan. He had to do what he could to learn if he could obtain any business or legal traction here. He began by going to the Department of Mines, which he found in a low-ceilinged concrete-block building on the edge of town. Wooden map-filing shelves lined the walls and large tables filled the center of the room, strewn with mining maps. A small, thin gray-haired man greeted him, first in Spanish, then realizing *no comprendo*, went on in English, "How may I assist you, sir."

Parke told his story and the man listened with polite attentiveness. "I know the properties you speak of. I can show you on the maps," he said and began rifling through the stacks of folios while they continued to talk. "It is believed these mines still have much to offer with the necessary capital investment."

They spent the afternoon looking over plat maps and mineral maps uninterrupted by anyone. Parke learned much about the locations, depths, extent of previous excavations, and prospects for these mines. Sensing the man's kindness and sincerity, as well as his knowledge and experience, Parke invited him to have dinner that evening at the hotel, which he graciously accepted.

"Wait, I don't even know your name," Parke said, and they both chuckled.

"I am Juan Paleo Romero, at your service," he said with an exaggerated elaborate bow.

Parke smiled. "I will meet you in the hotel dining room at 7:00 p.m."

After a short nap and a cool wash in his room, Parke arrived in the dining room to find Juan already there waiting. They ordered wine and spicy pork and cabbage *empanadas*.

"Have you lived here all your life?" Parke asked.

"I was born in a small village not far from here and came to labor in the mines when I was thirteen. On Sundays, I would visit my mother, sisters, and brothers in the village and bring them food for the week to supplement their fruit and nuts from the jungle and eggs from the chickens they kept. I always brought flour for *tortillas* and lard from the butcher shop. Sometimes, there were also meat scraps I could afford. Wages were low, and the work was hard, but I grew strong." He chuckled. "I know that may be difficult to believe seeing me now. I was always small, but I did get strong in those years.

"I made friends with the supervisors and one, in particular, took a liking to me and helped me. He taught me much about his job running the crews, who to call when the vein shifted, and how to redirect the work. He taught me English and made me speak it when I was with him. He introduced me to the older men who had much experience and they showed me better ways to do my job efficiently and more safely. The mines, in those days, were even more dangerous than today. Collapsed shafts, falling rocks, and accidental detonations killed men. The church bell would ring for an hour and everyone would stop working to pay respect.

"Over the years, I worked at several different mines and grew to know many in the mining community. I learned who was most skilled and trustworthy and how to avoid troublemakers. Eventually, I made friends with one of the mapmakers. He worked side-by-side with the mineralogists and created many of the maps at the Department of Mines. I became his apprentice and eventually they hired me to manage the map collection. It has been my life's work."

Juan and Parke ordered more wine and talked into the evening. Juan saw that Parke had many business-related questions he could not answer, but he offered to introduce him to some of the mine owners who were currently in town. Most lived abroad and only visited occasionally. Parke gratefully accepted his offer to make introductions and they parted amiably to talk further the next day.

In the late morning, Parke stopped by Juan's office.

"Greetings, my friend," Juan began. "I have exceptional news. This morning, Mr. Cambria came in to look over some maps. He is a major mine owner here and keeps a house for when he visits from London. I told him about you and he asked me to extend an invitation for you to come to his home this evening. He is planning to dine with Mr. Hernandez, who is another mine owner. Hernandez is from Spain."

As Juan talked, he wrote down the address and drew a crude map to the house for Parke. After his horrible experience at the palace, Parke was starting to feel better. He seemed to be on a solid path to learn about this place, the mining industry here, and to find out if he had a worthy opportunity or not.

That afternoon, he visited his mare at the stable to make sure she was cared for properly. While there, he noticed a man loading a cart for departure. He quickly went to his room and wrote to Ginger.

November 8, 1939

Darling Ginger,

I am so sorry this endeavor is taking longer than expected. I do think I have had a breakthrough though and will be meeting some prominent mine owners this evening to learn what I can. It is still unclear what our real prospects here might be. My goal is to leave soon and make my way back to you and our precious children. I hope you are all well and that you will be in my arms soon.

You are ever in my thoughts,

P.

He addressed an envelope and jogged back to the stable in time to put the note in the man's hand with *pesos* for postage. This would go out quicker than waiting for the weekly outgoing mail.

Evening came with a cooling breeze as Parke made his way to the Cambria address, turning down streets with the map in hand. When he arrived, he was impressed to find a modest but stately colonial-style home with a broad front porch and balcony above. A low fence and flowers surrounded the front yard and kitchen herbs grew in abundance. He ascended the front steps and crossed to the front door to ring the bell. A small, native woman opened the door wordlessly and ushered him into a drawing room where the two men sat in overstuffed chairs chatting amiably.

"Hello! Welcome," said the man seated facing him. He stood and extended a large hand to Parke. "You must be Mr. Lusk. I am John Cambria and this is my friend, Louis Hernandez." Hernandez also stood and shook Parke's hand warmly. "We are glad to meet a man who shares our passion for progress in this country."

Both men looked to be in their late fifties, with round bellies extolling their affluence. The servant brought mint julips with fresh mint from the garden. They moved to comfortable rocking chairs on the front porch to enjoy the slight breeze.

John began by telling of his twenty years of running mining operations in Wales and in Honduras for the past nine years. Louis shared his own background, which brought him first to Mexico and then south to Honduras. "Juan told me about your connection to Burke," said John. "The Burke holdings are noteworthy. What are your plans?"

"Well, I am uncertain of my footing here. A man named Hawkins, who I came to Honduras to meet, died two days ago of malaria. He was the executor of Burke's estate. He worked for years on settling the estate and was once thrown in prison."

"Wait. What?" John and Louis asked in unison. "How on earth did that happen?"

"It was this president. Tiburcio. Hawkins was friendly with the past president, Baraona, who had known Burke. Because Baraona had made promises to Burke that Hawkins wanted Tiburcio to honor."

"Ha! Well, now that clears things up," Louis laughed. "You cannot expect anything to transfer from one leader to another, especially here. Especially when they are from opposite parties."

"What were the promises?" asked John.

"They related to tax burdens," Parke replied.

"My friend, you do not need to worry about that," said Louis. "Yes, of course, if you make money in this country, there will be taxes to pay, but it is very easy to present plausible books to the government that are to your advantage. It is done all the time."

Parke paused and took a long deep breath. "It sounds like Hawkins perhaps spent a lot of time obsessing about the wrong thing, then."

They sat in silence for a moment listening to the sounds of the jungle coming to life at dusk.

"So, will you be starting things up here?" John asked.

"Well, I would appreciate some advice about what sort of capital and expertise it may require to get even one of Burke's mines back up and running."

"Expertise is easy to come by here," said Louis. "There are specialists throughout this community eager to work and labor is readily available. This is why the government does not bother us much. We bring employment to the men and boys of this country. You can find them for little pay, but if you want loyalty and employees you can trust, you must pay fare wages. Sometimes, room and board are required and medical care to those in need is important. If sickness sweeps through your work crews, you will lose time and money. You will see. Done correctly, you can earn back your investment and begin showing profits within the first year or two."

Parke liked these honest, successful businessmen. He wanted to be like them. "Can you give me an idea how much capital is needed to get started?"

"Well, what do you have to start with?" John asked.

Parke took a long moment. He did not want them to think he was naïve. He also did not want them to know he barely had enough to make this trip.

"I have some resources of my own," he ventured, "but I will mostly rely on investors. I have some leads on this I intend to pursue when I'm back in the states. But I do need an idea of what is needed."

The two men looked at each other and hesitated. Then, John said, "You should plan on at least $250,000.00 for each mine... $300,000.00 would be safer. Maybe you just start with one and see how it goes, but beyond capital you must understand you need a lot of luck. It is never a certainty that your mine will produce as expected or that your vein will not simply runout. Nothing is certain. That is why finding investors may be a challenge for you."

These words hit home for Parke. What was he thinking? He did not know. He wanted to be alone to sort out his feelings. The evening continued with small talk over dinner about news back in Europe and the global economy in general. Parke thought how his younger brother would likely be able to participate in this conversation, but Parke was mostly lost. He won favor by being witty and expounding on the lovely meal of fine Honduran dishes, which included vegetable soup with hot chiles and lime, *carne asada*, spicy rice and beans with goat cheese, *tortillas*, and banana cake for dessert. Parke took his leave as the other men retired to the porch for cigars. As they bid good evening, a white bat flew past the porch, brilliant in the evening gloom.

In the morning, Parke learned that Jesus had taken another guiding opportunity and was gone. He secured the services of a new *mozo* for the return trip to San Pedro and then on to

Puerto Cortes. The following day, he saddled up his mare and they began the journey.

⁂

G INGER WAS EXPECTING PARKE to be home in Pleasant Valley before the holidays and she was busy beginning to prepare for Christmas. She made new pillowcases for the girls, each embroidered with colorful flowers and their names. She knit scarves for the cousins and wool socks for the men. They celebrated Thanksgiving at Mimi's with all the family together, except one. Ellie outdid herself with two enormous turkeys dressed with sausage and apple stuffing, honey-glazed ham, mountains of potatoes mashed with sour cream and chives, roasted butternut squash, Brussels sprouts smothered in brown butter, light and fluffy yeast rolls, and three kinds of pie: pumpkin, peach, and blueberry.

The weather turned days afterwards and the wind blew the remaining leaves off the trees. Baba made her date nut candy in preparation for Christmas and rolled it up in a white dishtowel to age in the kitchen drawer. Closer to Christmas, she recruited everyone for a taffy-pull day. After boiling the sugar mixture to a hard crack stage, she poured it out to cool. If she started too soon, her hands burned beet red, but maybe that was part of the secret to the airiest, crispiest taffy in the world. With Ginger and the girls, Baba stretched out the long clumps of soft, warm taffy until it would almost come apart then fold it back repeatedly. The timing was crucial. Flavors included molasses, along with peppermint and spearmint from Ginger's garden harvest extracts.

Finally, Ginger received the letter from Parke that he was preparing to return to Puerto Cortes and arrange passage by sea to New Orleans. With the slowness of the mail, she was anticipating he could arrive any day. She was so relieved. It seemed as if he had been gone for a very long time and she missed him terribly. Allen was worried, too, and kept in close touch with Ginger, as did Mimi. There had been news in the paper about a late-season hurricane in November and they wondered if it had been the reason for the delayed mail... and possibly Parke's journey home.

As Christmas approached, Kate and Maggie were feeling sad. It just would not be Christmas without the cheer of their daddy. Kate continued to ask Ginger for more information about her father's mysterious voyage but her mother had little to offer. Ginger was now deeply distressed and started to wonder why exactly he did go there. She started drinking earlier in the day and would often be in bed by the time the girls came home from school. Baba cooked the meals and tried to get Ginger to eat. Sometimes, Ginger, in her derangement, hurled abusive epithets at her, which hurt and distressed Baba, bringing on pectoris angina pains in her chest and arm. Kate heard her moaning in the night and brought her nitroglycerin tablets. Baba also had spells of headaches for which she took empirin compound or the stronger codeine tablets. Sometimes, Kate felt responsible for taking care of everyone.

Baba and Ginger picked the girls up on Christmas Eve and they went to Mimi's house. Though everyone tried hard to be merry, it was the quietest Christmas Eve ever. The conversation repeatedly turned back to speculating about Parke, often in whispers so the children would not hear. Ginger was barely able to hold back tears. When she said goodnight to Mimi, they shared a long embrace. Mimi said, "Worrying has never done any good. It won't change anything, except make you sick. Have faith, dear."

On the way home, tears slid down Ginger's cheeks. She surreptitiously wiped them away under cover of darkness hoping Baba and the girls would not notice. She spoke up and participated in their conversation as though she was fine. Her nose ran and she was sniffling, but she brushed it off to them as some sort of allergy, perhaps to Mimi's scented candles. Nevertheless, they all knew she was not fine. Parke was the center of their well-being. Without him to fill their sails, they were adrift in a still sea.

TWO WEEKS LATER, THE snow had melted in a January thaw and Clifford was outside on Mimi's lawn raking leaves in balmy fifty-degree weather. Clifford's wife hated that he smoked, but his employer did not seem to mind, so he took advantage of the relative privacy of the side yard to smoke a Chesterfield. The gardener leaned on his rake and enjoyed the warmth of the winter sun against his wool sweater. He had shed his coat, hat, and gloves after the first fifteen minutes of work. When his cigarette was finished, he flicked the butt to the side, and resumed his work. Earlier that day, while fetching tools from the basement, he had cracked open a basement window a few inches to air out the musty smell, intending to close it before heading home.

In a devastatingly unlikely coincidence, the cigarette butt flew straight into that small opening and landed on a small gasoline spill under the lawn mower gas can. The still-hot butt immediately ignited the spill, which, in turn, ignited some storage boxes. Clifford had walked around the house by then and did not see the flames or smell the smoke. As the flames spread, they eventually found the paint cans, turpentine, and beams that supported the center of the house. At 2:27 p.m. on that January day, an explosion rocked the house.

Mimi and Agnes had been at the back of the house with Ellie, watching her make macaroons and having a cup of tea. They all flew to the back door and escaped before the second explosion broke through the living room floorboards, spreading flames up the drapes and across the wallpaper. Within minutes, the house was a raging inferno. The neighbors summoned the Davenport Fire Department, but it was another fifteen minutes before the sound of sirens approached.

Clifford moved the car from the driveway to the other side of the street, where the neighbor ushered them all inside to watch from their large front windows. Ellie sat on the sofa and wept uncontrollably with her hands to her face while Clifford tried to calm her down. Agnes stood next to Mimi looking out the window, hiccupping noisily. Mimi stood still and silent, stoically taking it all in. The fire department was only able to help ensure that the neighboring residences were watered and kept safe. Clifford left after a few hours and walked home to his wife and dinner. The house and its contents burned all night, filling the neighborhood with acrid smoke.

Homecoming

THE FIRE WAS DEVASTATING. Mimi went to stay at Dottie's house, where she could borrow some clothes and decide what to do next. Allen had paid the insurance annually after his father's death, so there would be some compensation eventually. The loss of all the memorabilia from their lives, however, was a jagged pill to swallow. Moreover, nothing could ever truly replace that grand home. Agnes was put on a bus to live with her sister in Des Moines. Both Mimi and Ellie saw her off with the last of her wages. Mimi employed her nine years. The flames had consumed all her earthly possessions, seemingly safely tucked away in her attic room.

That evening when they got home, Parke saw the struggle on her face. He poured her a small glass of wine in honor of her birthday, which infuriated Maggie. "When you are a bit older, little one," Parke said. This delighted Kate to no end.

Mimi wanted to keep Ellie in her employment and asked Dottie if she could stay on as long as Mimi lived there. Dottie was somewhat put off by the idea. After all, whatever would she do with her time if there were someone else managing her kitchen and feeding her family? Besides singing in church and rearing children, her interests did not warrant more free time. Finally, Mimi conceded that it would be uncomfortable for her daughter and provided excellent references to help Ellie find a new position. After some asking around, the stylish Hotel Blackhawk hired Ellie to cook for the daily breakfast and lunch shifts. As the tastes of the high-end clients ran to delicacies and extravagance for special occasions, Ellie hoped to work her way into the catering chef position eventually. Ellie had dreamed of this since she was a girl learning to cook with her mother, aunt, and grandmother. She was happy to have an opportunity and grateful to Mimi for the glowing referral.

As for Mimi, she needed time to think about all that had happened. There did not seem to be a big hurry, since Dottie had the extra space. She would ask Allen his opinion. She had just turned sixty-five and, with Harry gone, maybe she did not need to own a home. Maybe she should rent something small and easy to care for on her own. What would Parke say? She hoped with all she had that she would be able to know his thoughts face-to-face again soon. She said a prayer that night before bed, wishing him safe passage, from wherever he was, back to where he belonged.

Meanwhile, Ginger spent time drinking, sleeping, and staring at the horizon out the window. Kate tried to cheer her up.

"Mama, let me do your nails for you. The fancy way you showed me."

"What for?"

"For something for me to do and something for you to feel good about."

Without further conversation, Kate brought the hand lotion, pumice stone, clippers, cuticle snippers, and bottles of polish. She slipped off her mother's house slippers and put her feet in a pan of warm water to soak. Then, she cleaned and moisturized her mother's hands, used a pumice stone on her calluses and carefully shaped her nails and cuticles, taking deliberate time on each finger. With all the care that Ginger had taught her, she slowly and carefully colored the half-moon at the base to match the white outer nail in creamy white polish and the middle with cherry red. She gave both colors two coats, plus a clear coat on top. She did the same on her feet and toes. Once, Kate made eye contact with Baba who was working in the kitchen. She nodded her head in approval to Kate. Ginger needed whatever they could give her, anything to keep her from sinking below the waves.

Two days later, Kate and Maggie arrived home from school to find their mother, once again, asleep in bed in the late afternoon. Kate helped Baba finish making dinner and they attempted to wake Ginger to join them. As Baba and the girls sat down at the table to eat, they heard footsteps on the front porch and all turned at once to see the front door open. There stood Parke, smiling broadly and holding the reins of a gray mare, staring at them all curiously. Kate reached him first, throwing her arms around his neck and squeezing tight. Maggie joined her. Then Ginger came out of the bedroom and stared in disbelief. She was in a rumpled dress and her hair was askew.

She said, "Parke Lusk. I don't know if I should kiss you or slap you."

He looked slightly confused and then replied, "I would prefer the former."

She teetered toward him, unsteady on her feet, and kissed him hard on the mouth. Then, she stepped back, balled up her small fist and punched him square on the jaw. It felt like she broke her hand. He grabbed her and held her tight in his arms, whispering in her ear. "Ginger, baby. Are you okay? Whatever is wrong?"

After a few minutes of everyone talking simultaneously, they finally regrouped. Kate went with Parke to get the horse settled, which included fetching hay from Dodie's barn, Ginger went to comb her hair and put on lipstick, and nine-year old Maggie jumped up and down squealing. Finally, they all sat together, Ginger snuggling into Parke's side so close, with her hand wrapped in a dishtowel filled with ice, she was almost lost under his protective arm. Parke began his story, corroborated in two days by the letters he had sent. They arrived all at once—and much behind schedule.

"I rode the horse all the way back to Puerto Cortes rather than take the train I had traveled on the first day of the journey. I needed to get the horse settled and decide what to do with her. We had become good companions and I was loath to leave her in the hands of someone like her former owner. After stabling her, I went to check on Hawkins' wife. The labyrinth of alleyways proved too confusing and I got lost. When I finally made it back to the docks, I asked a boy, he was about ten years old, to take me to her address. I rang the bell, but there was no answer. I found my way back to the dock again and had a bowl of *sopa de caracol*. I will teach you how to make it, so delicious. It has fresh conch and coconut, but I think it would be good with any seafood we can get from the riverboats. Anyway, after a good night's sleep, I returned to the Hawkins' place, on my own this time, and found Mrs. Hawkins at home.

"She was in a bad state. The last of her funds had paid for her husband's burial. She cried as we sat in her inner courtyard and my heart broke for her. I was also getting desperately short on funds but knew I had to help her. I ended up buying her passage to Houston and giving her money for a bus to her hometown from there. In exchange, she said I could stay at the house in Puerto Cortes, since the rent was paid-up through the end of the month. This was in November. The arrangement gave me time to figure out what I needed to do next.

"The busiest part of town was the docks and I spent time there each day, talking with boat captains and dock workers, looking for an angle I could follow to secure some funds. Luck was with me. I befriended a merchant, John Garrett, who shipped merchandise back and forth between Puerto Cortes and various ports around the gulf, including Tampa, New Orleans, and Houston. He was having trouble with what looked like theft, but he could not be sure. His captains reported missing merchandise, spoilage thrown overboard, and other anomalies that seemed nefarious. He asked me if I would serve as ship chandler for his company until his brother, Paul, returned in early January. His brother had recently married and he and his bride were on a honeymoon in Europe.

"I greeted three vessels weekly, checked in all of their cargo, and then documented everything loaded for departure the following day. He paid me well. I arranged with the landlord to secure the Hawkins residence through mid-January and moved my mare to a better stable where she received oats and a pasture to graze. She immediately began to put on weight and show her true beauty. As time went on, I realized I would earn enough in two months to secure passage for both myself and the mare, which, by then, I named Donabella."

At the conclusion of his story, Baba insisted Parke call his mother. It was at that moment they all realized he did not know about the fire or that Mimi was staying at Dottie's house. When they explained, once again all talking at once, Parke was ashen. He called and talked with Mimi and she said she would tell the rest of the family of his safe return and they would all see him tomorrow. Then, just after he hung up the phone, Kate remembered to tell him about Buck.

They all went to bed that night feeling so much relief, except for Parke. Well, yes, he was happy to see his family and to be in their embrace. More importantly, he was happy to be there for them, feeling a certain amount of guilt over being gone during the holidays, not being there when Buck reached the end of his life, and not being there to console and support his family. But the fire... that was a blow that would take much time to process.

The next morning, Parke and Ginger dropped the girls off at school and then drove to the homesite on Brady Street. They parked the car and walked around the ruin. There was nothing much to speak of: the chimney and charred remains of the black marble mantle, a fragment of some piece of furniture that may have been his parent's headboard, and some books still retaining their form against all odds, completely black. Parke was silent and moved as though he was underwater, his shoulders bearing the burden of loss.

They then drove to Dottie's house. Unbelievably, Mimi seemed unchanged by the disaster. She was chipper, joking, and teasing her son about scaring the living daylights out of poor Ginger. Parke left the living room to refill his mother's teacup in the kitchen. There, he spoke with Dottie.

"You think Mom is truly okay?"

"She is doing better than any of us. She said it was God's will and that was fine with her," Dottie confirmed.

Parke gazed out into the other room watching her interact and laugh with Ginger. "Amazing," he said, shaking his head in disbelief.

They stopped for lunch at the Blackhawk and waved to Ellie through the kitchen door. She was too busy to come out, but raised her voice over the clatter of pots and pans to say, "So glad you are alive and well, Mr. Lusk!"

"Me, too!" he shouted back with a warm smile.

They ordered steak and French fries, Parke's favorite comfort food. The steak was cooked to juicy perfection and the fries were salted just right. "I love American food," exclaimed Parke.

After lunch, they went by the office to catch up with Allen, who greeted Parke warmly with a handshake and said, "Good to have you safely home, brother."

They sat in his large back office, Allen on the corner of his desk, and Parke and Ginger seated in overstuffed wingback chairs. Parke told his story again with details about what had happened, including Hawkins' death, and why he was delayed returning. They talked about Mimi and marveled together at her constitution. Allen said it would likely be several months, maybe up to six, before she would begin receiving any insurance money.

"They have to investigate. Make sure it wasn't arson. This will take time. And, of course, insurance companies want to hold onto their money for long as possible before conceding," he explained.

"How is everything here?" Parke asked, looking around the office and glancing out at the other employee desks. Everyone was still at lunch celebrating a secretary's birthday.

"The two of us should go over things tomorrow after you have had time to rest," Allen answered.

"If you think you can't talk business in front of Ginger, you best give it up," Parke protested. "She has exclaimed that I will never again be out of her sight."

And with that, Ginger crossed her arms and gave Allen a quick, deliberate nod, thereby standing her ground.

Allen laughed and said, "Alright then. Duly noted." He took a breath and a moment to gather his words.

"I have been realizing lately that our industry is changing. National syndicated chains are putting some of the small grocers out of business. Because of their high volume, they can offer lower prices. I believe this trend will continue building momentum and we need to think ahead. I have begun keeping the books for the Davenport Candy Company on the side. It has eaten into some of my family time, but Marybeth understands. In any case, it has been a revelation. The Coin brothers have done an amazing job of bringing in the most modern and efficient equipment. A fireproof building protects everything. Smart! Their product has a longer shelf life than anything we sell and they are selling in high volume to the syndicated chains. It's all brilliant."

"What does that have to do with us?" Parke asked.

"Well, I am very interested in getting involved. Either as a manager or an investor."

"Investor? Do you have that much money stashed away," Parke asked, incredulous.

"Well, no. But it could be raised if we sold Lusk & Sons."

"Wow. Really? You are ready to walk away from what Dad and Granddad built?"

"Maybe. I am just thinking aloud, but it could be a smart move... and lucrative for us. It will be very interesting to see what the war in Europe does to our economy. The U.S. is now providing supplies to the Allies, which is creating growth here." Allen was a genius with numbers and Parke had no reason to doubt him.

This was, however, a sharp departure from what Parke wanted to discuss. He felt it was time to put his proposal forward.

"Actually, I have news to share from Honduras and you may be interested in the family's prospects there. We have opportunities. Many of the worries Hawkins had were complicated by his illness. He had also become paranoid after his imprisonment—not that I can blame him in that regard. I spoke with the Department of Mines and other mine owners. They helped me understand what it would take to get our mines operating again."

Allen stared at him for a long moment. "How much capital?"

"Between $250,000.00 and $300,000.00 per mine, an investment which could be returned within two years."

Ginger turned her head and stared at her husband as if he may have lost his mind. Allen whistled a long, slow exhale. "Brother, where on earth are we going to get that much money?"

"Well, I have an idea that we can go up to Chicago, or maybe even New York, and talk to investors," Parke said. He reached over and took Ginger's hand without looking at her, because he knew she would object to him going anywhere.

They talked a bit longer and finally decided there was much to think about. Parke and Ginger picked up the girls from school and they all went home to enjoy Baba's meatloaf with mashed potatoes and gravy.

After dinner, Parke and Kate went to the barn to feed Donabella. "Isn't she a beauty, honey? You should have seen her when I first found her. The fella who had her won her in a card game. He was a sodden drunk with no idea about horses. There was no way I was leaving her there."

"Is she a good riding horse?" Kate asked.

"Oh, you just wait. She is so smart and eager to please." Parke gave Kate a warm smile and held her gaze. "It's so good to see you again!" He noticed how much she had grown in such a short time.

"I had the most absurd saddle to ride while I was there, but I picked this one up during the last week in Honduras." He showed her a well-oiled Australian stock saddle. She had never seen one.

He continued explaining. "It is a great combination of the swell and cantle of a Western saddle to hold you firm, with English stirrups... which are so much better on the knees."

"Can't wait to try it, Dad," Kate exclaimed, clearly wanting his approval.

That spring and summer of 1940, Parke and Kate spent much time working with the new horse, teaching her how to bow and spin around on cue. She was fun to ride and Kate spent many otherwise idle hours playing around with her.

Ginger, meanwhile, kept Parke on a short leash. He wrote letters to investment companies and researched ways to raise capital. Allen and Parke talked many times about a trip to Chicago, but daily life at home kept them busy. Parke had to get his accounts all caught up. Others in the office covered for him in his absence, but many small accounts had suffered. He did as much as possible over the phone and only took a few short trips. Weekends were, once again, spent at the club. Things slowly got back to normal.

Except Parke started having frequent nightmares. They were always about the family home on Brady Street. The content varied. Sometimes, he was a boy, living with his young parents. Sometimes, Billy Velie was there, his old amiable self. Other times, he was entertaining friends on the front porch on a hot summer day. Regardless of what happened in the dream, he woke with his heart pounding and a tightness in his chest.

Each time, it was like realizing for the first time that the house was gone. He felt he had lost something valuable and very specific to himself. These dreams disturbed him because they would not cease. He felt haunted by the house itself. Once, he talked to his mother about the dreams. She promised to think and pray on it and see if she could help him find some peace in discovering what the dreams meant.

In November, they gathered for Thanksgiving at Dottie's house, which was a huge change for the family. Instead of Ellie and Agnes presenting the finished fare, Dottie, Ginger, and Baba cooked it all, starting at 7:00 in the morning. Extra chairs from Allen's house and tables from various rooms at Dottie's combined to make one long surface, extending from the dining room into the living room. Everyone crowded in. Mimi asked Parke to say grace. As an agnostic, Parke took no stock in trying to talk to God. He did, however, enjoy holding court, being chosen for the task over his brother, and having everyone at the table being of like mind... if only for a few moments. He was not about to disappoint his mother.

"Dear Lord, thank you for the blessing of this family gathering and our good health. Bless the people fighting and enduring the horrible war in Europe. Keep them strong and bring peace to their ravaged souls. Help us always remember those less fortunate and guide us in helping them in your name. Amen."

It was a lovely, leisurely meal. The adults shared wine, the cousins played hide-and-seek, and everyone took turns working a large puzzle of a European castle.

When Christmas rolled around it was another stark reminder of how the fire had changed their lives. They gathered at Allen's house on Christmas Eve, exchanged gifts and ate hors d'oeuvres that had been ordered in from the restaurant the day before. Ellie herself prepared the order: small roast beef sandwiches, individual minced meat pies made in muffin tins, deviled eggs, dried fruit dipped in dark chocolate, and salted roasted nuts. How things had changed. Parke had the family home by 7:30 p.m.

Kate turned thirteen in January 1941. The next year flew by and Kate and Alice were inseparable. They spent as much time together as their parents would allow working on their riding skills and school studies. Over the summer, they both began competing in jumping and dressage matches. Kate was getting tall and Ginger had to keep making new pants for her competitions. She was five-foot-eight-inches tall and self-conscious that she towered over her mother and younger sister. Her instinct was to slouch and make herself blend in, but Ginger and Baba rebuked her saying she must always "stand up straight, shoulders back, neck long." She was also developing a curvy figure, requiring a new style of underclothes that chaffed, restricted, and embarrassed her when Ginger and Baba talked about it.

The following fall, Kate and Alice started public high school together. Kate's favorite class was English where they read books, discussed them, and wrote essays. She would spend hours writing and rewriting her papers, finding the best way to turn a phrase for the best effect. The classes were much larger and she and Alice drifted apart as they made new friends.

Kate was also keenly interested in the boys and gravitated toward opportunities to fraternize and joke with them in the halls. They, in turn, were all attracted to her long, strawberry-blond hair and voluptuous shape. She did not have a boyfriend, as such, but many boys were her friends who kept her dance card full at school socials through the fall.

On the evening of December 7, snow was falling. Kate and Maggie had homework and Parke helped them, as needed, while also reading a book. Baba was mending and Ginger was knitting a sweater but refused to say whom it was for. Then, a radio announcement interrupted the program with news of the bombing of Pearl Harbor. They all looked at the atlas and tried to measure how far Hawaii was from Iowa. The seriousness of it all did not escape anyone.

The next day, President Roosevelt declared war on Japan and the United States entered World War II. At school, boys in the upper classes were enraged and many asked their parent's permission to enlist even though they were not of age. Parents who had served in World War I were much more likely to allow their sons to join up early at only seventeen years old. The school hallway volume noticeably diminished as some of the most popular athletes said their goodbyes and headed to boot camp. The older girls begged them to write and promised to write back. There were tearful goodbyes. The boys in Kate's classes were jealous, claiming they could fight as well as anyone. Kate was afraid for everyone. The school implemented monthly air raid drills because of the arms factory in Davenport. They all had to jump to the floor and crawl under their desks. Kate imagined the building all blown to pieces with nothing left but the desks keeping the children safe. She was highly skeptical. It occurred to her that by the time she was of age, all the eligible boys would have died in the stupid, senseless war.

As Kate's fourteenth birthday approached, Ginger made arrangements for Kate and a few friends to have an evening sleigh ride out over the country club grounds to a place in the woods where a bonfire would be built. They would have hot chocolate and roast marshmallows. At 5:30 p.m., after all had eaten dinner at home, the girls met in front of the country club to find two beautiful draft horses hitched to an antique sleigh.

Fur robes blanketed them against the chill as they all squeezed into the back. Kate was a bit miffed that Ginger allowed Maggie to come, but her mother insisted, saying it was only fair. They sang caroling songs and had fun. Unfortunately, Maggie, as usual, stole the show with her antics. Kate tried not to show it, but this put her in a bad mood. The day no longer felt like hers.

She dug deep to try to understand why she and Maggie were not close. All she came up with is plain sheer jealousy. Maggie was cute, bubbly, funny, and the apple of her mother's eye. Though the family marveled at the beautiful color of Kate's hair, her excellent grades, and natural riding abilities, Kate thought it was a consolation prize. She felt like she was somehow second best, even despite her father's obvious love and affection for her. She also knew it was wrong for her to have these feelings.

That evening when they got home, Parke saw the struggle on her face. He poured her a small glass of wine in honor of her birthday, which infuriated Maggie. "When you are a bit older, little one," Parke said. This delighted Kate to no end.

Big Business

W HEN SPRING ROLLED AROUND, Parke was very aware that more than two years had passed since his return from what the family called his "expedition." In addition to retrieving old accounts that had gone stale, he had worked hard to build more business with the long-standing customers. He had also enlisted the assistance of a skilled carpenter to help him build an addition on the farmhouse. He received an immediate return on his investment with a happy family.

The business seemed to be on solid footing, so he was finally able to talk Allen into a trip together to Chicago's financial district. They left in the afternoon after booking a shared suite at the Palmer House Hotel by telephone. After checking in to their rooms, they went to the famous Chez Paree for dinner. The news reported that rationing was about to be implemented, but they arrived in Chicago before it began and thus splurged. They ordered bacon-wrapped filet mignon with wild mushrooms sautéed in a merlot reduction, potatoes *au gratin*, fresh spring asparagus in lemon *buerre blanc*, and warm popovers dripping with melted butter.

In the morning, they dressed in their best suits and, after grabbing a quick coffee and Danish, drove to the Rookery Building on LaSalle Street. Upon entering the large edifice, they found themselves immersed in light, surrounded by white marble, and faced with a staircase that rimmed the entire room spiraling upward to the other floors. An elevator was across the lobby, but they chose to take the stairs to enjoy the view of the architecture on their way up to the third floor where they had an appointment with Robert Duncan of Duncan-Smith Investing. An attractive young receptionist greeted them and invited them to make themselves comfortable in the waiting room. She then brought them each a large cup of hot coffee. After sipping their beverages and waiting for about thirty minutes, they both needed to relieve their bladders. Just then, the receptionist announced that Mr. Duncan was ready to see them.

They were ushered into a well-appointed office exuding wealth with a parquet floor, a massive, carved mahogany desk, dark leather chairs, and an intricate Art Deco chandelier. Mr. Duncan insisted they call him Robert and greeted them with an air of self-important, affected manners. He was immaculately dressed in a dark-gray-striped tweed, double-breasted suit, white shirt, and a maroon tie. After they took their seats, he cordially invited them to make their pitch. He sat listening attentively, fingertips spread and touching below his chin, making unblinking eye contact with each as they spoke. Allen had helped Parke design projection spreadsheets to show how things could go, at least hopefully.

When they were finished, Robert Duncan came straight to the point.

"You fellas have what could be a valuable property, at some point. But here is what you need to understand now. We are in the midst of a horrible war. Even a year before we entered the war, we were providing supplies to the Allies and all mining and production efforts turned to the metals needed for airplanes, jeeps, guns, helmets, and food tins for the troops. Now, if you had an iron mine for making steel, or if you had aluminum or tin, you would not even need to be here talking to me. The government would be at your door offering to finance your entire operation.

"The value of gold and silver has dropped significantly in the past two years. It is expected to further decline in value for the duration of this bloody war. I believe you will have a very difficult road finding investors. As for me, I cannot support your efforts at this time."

Parke and Allen sat in stunned silence for a few moments. They then rose and thanked him for his time. Mr. Duncan walked them to the door and gave them one last piece of advice.

"Since you made the long trip up here, you may want to stop by the Mercantile Exchange at Franklin and Washington. My secretary can give you directions. They keep up-to-the-minute track of values on both agricultural and mining futures. Best of luck to you."

The only good thing about the brevity of the meeting was that they could both use the men's room down the hall before their bladders burst. After that, they got the directions and drove off in silence to the seventeen-story Chicago Mercantile Exchange Building. They took the elevator to the second-story trading floor. There were about twenty people milling around watching the ticker tape machine readings, discussing prices and calculating their profits and losses. Parke and Allen asked who had a specialty in metals trading and were directed to a man in suspenders sitting at a desk along the wall. He emphatically supported the bad news alluded to by Mr. Duncan. He said that the gold and silver market had dropped a whopping twenty percent and the bottom would be nowhere in sight until the war was won or the world blew itself to pieces, whichever came first.

The brothers sat side-by-side on counter stools at the café across the street at mid-afternoon. The matronly waitress, old enough to be their mother, served them the blue-plate lunch special: creamed chipped beef on toast, coleslaw, and baked beans with a bottle of Coca Cola. They said little on the ride back home, pulling into Davenport at 7:00 p.m., just after sunset. Parke dropped by Dottie's house to tell Mimi the disappointing news.

"Well, at least you have some information now and aren't flying blind," said Mimi. They sat at the kitchen table having a cup of coffee. After giving Parke a moment to brood in silence, Mimi approached another topic.

"Are you still having upsetting dreams, son?"

Parke sighed. "Yes. At least once a week I wake with a sense of utter dread. The dreams always take place in our old house. Ginger is sympathetic but doesn't know what to make of it all."

Mimi offered some support. "I have been thinking about it a lot and I may have an idea," she started. "That house was special. It was like being royalty living in such a showcase home in the best part of town. I know your father got a lot of satisfaction out of bringing business associates there to show off his importance.

It occurs to me that we all derived stature from that home. Maybe you need to spend some time thinking about how this obsession with the mines in Honduras may be connected to a need for self-importance."

Although she delivered her message gently and lovingly, Parke still felt the sting. He promised to give it some thought and kissed her on the cheek before heading home.

The next day was Saturday and Kate confronted her parents at breakfast. Ginger had set the table with new dishes that she and Parke had picked out as a Christmas gift to each other. They were Ballerina Mist; a pale, seafoam green with a thin, silver band around the edge. They knew the war would make finer things scarce so they bought a big set including dinner plates, lunch plates, cups with saucers, and serving dishes with lids. At fifteen, Kate was highly emotional and keen to appreciate finer things. Those dishes seemed to elevate their lot in life. As Parke read the paper and Ginger and Baba flipped pancakes and fried bacon and eggs, Kate broached the subject.

"Daddy, can you please tell me what you and Uncle Allen were doing in Chicago? And, for that matter, I still don't know why you went to Honduras." She flashed her mother's back a scathing dirty look for keeping her in the dark.

Parke put down the paper, leaned forward with his arms on the table, and turned his head to look at her directly.

"Yes, honey. Of course, I will tell you. There are mines in Honduras that we seem to have inherited. They are gold and silver mines."

Kate's eyes got big and round and she looked over her shoulder at Maggie laying on the living room floor reading the comics and listening to the radio. She was pleased Maggie had not heard what he said.

"Does that mean we are rich?" she whispered.

He laughed a little. "No, far from it. You see, the only way to extract the minerals is with a lot of skilled men and heavy machinery, which is very, *very* expensive. That is the reason we went to Chicago. We talked to people about the price of gold and silver and looked into finding an investor to help us, but the war has caused the value of these precious metals to fall dramatically. It is just not the time to start up an operation like this."

"Oh," Kate said, defeated. She sat very still deep in thought.

Parke kept looking at her in case she had any questions. After a few silent moments, he went back to reading the paper.

For Kate, this information was fascinating in an exciting, disappointing, frustrating way—she was feeling all these emotions, all at the same time. It was almost more than she could bear to remain seated and finish breakfast. She went straight to the barn to think. While her thoughts spun, she brushed Donabella and worked the tangles out of her tail. Then, she plaited her mane in a dozen small braids to make it wavy when they came out. Donabella stood there patiently in the stall, even though her door to the pasture was open. Now and then, the mare would shift her weight and lean on Kate, who would have to push the horse's massive weight back to center. She put Vaseline around the horse's eyes to make them stand out and to deter biting flies. She briefly considered applying some to the mare's whither to evoke flying dreams. Finally, Kate gave her the carrot stashed in her pocket and shoved the animal out the door to graze.

Kate thought about how it must have been difficult for her parents to keep the secret from her and Maggie. Baba would have known and Mimi, too. Just *not* the kids. It was so intriguing. They must have imagined a completely new life for them all... maybe her parents even thought of living in Honduras! Her father said it was beautiful there. The entire notion was all just this ethereal thing, hanging out there in space, waiting for a different time. A time when people could have normal lives and not when all the eligible young men were dying. Eventually, she came back inside and joined Maggie in the living room reading comics.

Summer came and went and Kate started her sophomore year at school. The freshmen all looked too young to be there and she felt sorry for them wandering the halls, not sure what to do. There were a few new cute boys, too young for her, of course, but she would not hesitate to dance with them if they asked at the autumn social.

As the holiday season approached, there were five parties organized, some at large family homes, and a New Year's Eve ball at the country club. She would wear a kelly-green taffeta gown made by Ginger and Baba and a velveteen evening cape with a white rabbit fur collar and muff she received for Christmas. She dressed to the recording of Claude Thornhill's "Snowfall," while the snow lightly fell on the lawn. The music played on the tall gramophone inherited from Handsome Harry on which he played Caruso. It had to be wound up by hand before each 78-rpm record was played. Sometimes, it had to be cranked up part way through because the music got too slow.

Just as she finished dressing, Parke tapped lightly on the door and she invited him in.

"Oh, my beautiful girl. You look so grown up and sophisticated. I have something special for you. I know your sixteenth birthday isn't for another few weeks, but I want you to have this now for the ball."

He pulled a small, black-velvet box out of his coat pocket and slowly opened it so she could see what was inside. It was a gold ring set with garnets surrounded by tiny pearls. Kate gasped and threw her arms around her father's neck. It was the most beautiful thing she had ever seen. Garnets were not only her birthstone but also her absolute favorite gem.

"Next month we will have your Sweet Sixteen portrait taken at the studio in town," he promised.

Parke drove her for the portrait on the day of her birthday. She wore a white rayon button-front blouse with an embroidered collar that draped elegantly over her shoulders. Her long, strawberry-blonde hair, usually done up in a knot or braided for the barn, hung loose, framing her face. Ginger had trimmed her bangs that morning and showed her how to apply some of her red lipstick. She sat with her hands resting on a table in front of her, carefully arranged to show off the new dinner ring from her father.

Over the course of that school year, her parents had taken Harry's earlier advice and they wrote to different finishing schools for her to complete her studies. In 1944, she was granted an interview at Southern Seminary in Buena Vista, Virginia. Assuming the school would accept her after the formality of the interview, Ginger and Baba carefully packed her suitcase and Parke accompanied her on the train. The proprietors of the school, Mr. and Mrs. Robey interviewed all candidates for admission in what was once the Buena Vista Hotel, a three story, rambling Renaissance- and Queen Anne-style structure that looked to Kate like a castle. She had never imagined such a magnificent place to attend school. The Robey's were serious schoolmasters. They spoke of their values regarding etiquette, behavior, and the hard academic work expected of their students. Parke was charming and Kate was on her best and most polite behavior despite shaking with excitement inside. Parke gave her a long warm hug, kissed her on the forehead, and left her in the care of the Robeys.

She shared her dorm room with three other girls, Hattie, Elsie, and Bridget. Hattie was a big round girl from Georgia, the daughter of a pecan farmer. She was jolly and talkative and her accent made everything she said funny to the other girls. Elsie was a shy girl with large brown eyes and long dark hair from North Carolina whose father was a lawyer. Bridget was five feet tall and made up for her stature by being over confident and sometimes bossy. Her parents lived in New York City managing their properties, everything from inner-city office buildings, to houses out in the countryside and industrial farm land. Actually, Kate got the impression that the parents did not do much of anything except delegate management to a large staff. They spent their time "being seen" at the theater, the opera, art exhibit openings, and the best restaurants in the city. Bridget's up-to-the minute wardrobe was professionally hand-tailored. The four of them got along well despite their very different backgrounds. After lights out at 10:30 on school nights, they all stayed up late whispering while listening for Mrs. Robey's footsteps in the hallway. They discussed the sisterhood mystery of their synced menses cycles and shared information and misinformation about sex and childbirth.

Classes included art, literature, history, and etiquette. Literature was Kate's favorite, but she also liked history. She worked hard to take the teacher's advice of learning the sequence of events that made up time, rather than the tedious task of remembering specific dates. Etiquette was annoying but a requirement of the curriculum. Young ladies needed to behave in a manner becoming their gender, entertain guests, know how to negotiate awkward social situations, attract a successful husband, and raise their children to be pillars of the community. The teacher caught Kate daydreaming in this class more than once.

The best part about Southern Seminary, besides the beautiful architecture and grounds, was that there were stables. Riding, as well as French, were electives, only enjoyed by a small set. The boys school nearby shared the stables with Southern Seminary. It was the only common ground where the young men and women could fraternize unescorted. Ten well-mannered riding horses were stabled there, with a riding arena for lessons, and miles of trails through the Virginia countryside. Kate, naturally, spent much time there.

On Sundays, the girls were all expected at church and then to spend time writing home to their families or gathering for high tea in the afternoon, but Saturdays were theirs. They could walk the half-mile to town and go to the soda shop, cinema, five-and-dime store, hair salon, or whatever. The catch was that the girls of Southern Seminary had to exhibit well-bred manners consistent with the rules of their school. This included wearing skirts or dresses, stylish hats, and white gloves... gloves at all times. Even in the heat of the sweltering Virginia humidity. This was too much for Kate. She only accompanied her roommates twice to town to see movies at the theater. The second time, Mrs. Robey herself caught her sauntering down the main street with no hat or gloves. She received a summons to the office and received a harsh reprimand, noted in her official school records. Her off-campus privileges were revoked for two weeks.

Though she exhibited perfect remorse in front of Mrs. Robey, Kate stormed back to her room in a fury. Her room-mates marveled at her nerve to break the rules. They begged her to behave; such infractions could result in dismissal from Southern Seminary. As for Kate, she was restless, bored, and finding this fancy school tedious. She made up her mind to avoid going to town even after the two weeks. She would spend her idle hours in the stable playing with the horses, wearing jeans, boots, and flannel shirts. Finally, she realized that Mrs. Robey's punishment was like throwing the proverbial rabbit into the briar patch, just what she wanted. She did write to her parents but never mentioned the incident. They were so proud she was attending Southern Seminary and Kate wanted to please them, but her inner mood was swinging toward rebellion.

After several Saturdays spent at the stables and out on the trails, she made two special new friends, Hector and Lucas. They were cousins and best friends and the same age as Kate. They came from a small town in Kentucky where their families raised thoroughbreds. Hector had a ridiculous shock of red hair that always wanted to stand straight up in cowlicks. He was tall and covered in freckles. Lucas was almost as tall and had brown hair and dimples.

They loved to play tricks on each other and always told Kate about it beforehand so she was in on the joke. One of these was to untie each other's horses so the other had to go catch the horse; sometimes easy and sometimes a challenge. Teasing about not knowing how to tie up a damned horse inevitably followed. Another was to hide each other's favorite tack, so the other one and Kate left them behind to catch up. They made her laugh and challenged her to races across the grounds. Her favorite horse was Roy, a seventeen-hand Standardbred that made her feel literally on top of the world in the saddle.

She cherished their time together and waited all week to see them. Her roommates teased her about being sweet on the boys, but she did not mind. Their time together was the highlight of the week and soothed her soul with simple pleasures of comradery, physical exercise, fresh air, and nature. A Thanksgiving celebration at the school was available for those unable to travel home for the long weekend. All her roommates, as well as Hector and Lucas, received train and bus tickets to get home, but her parents said they would have her come for Christmas holiday. Thanksgiving was an extravagance.

She spent the long weekend mostly by herself. The other girls who stayed were organizing games and popcorn parties, but she decided to simply catch up on all her studies and even get a little ahead. She was also working on redesigning a dress to wear to the Christmas ball to which the boys' school was invited. It was a grand affair featuring a live orchestra, candlelit tables, and a banquet with inspired dishes, as rationing would allow.

Just before Christmas break, the date arrived with much noise in the hallways as the girls spent the entire day readying themselves. Manicures, hair setting, dress altering for the perfect fit, and polishing of jewelry. When the time came, Mr. Robey announced each girl as she appeared at the top of the stairs to descend to the ballroom floor. Kate felt nervous and exceptionally vulnerable. She felt as if this was part of their "training" for society and it chaffed her in a way she could not explain.

Within moments, Hector and Lucas appeared, relieving all of her stress, and soon they were competing in comical ways to bring her punch and dance with her. They had a lovely evening, the three of them. The highlight of the night was stepping outside to cool off in the night air and seeing the Milky Way strewn across the deep black sky. As they gazed, a shooting star made a perfect arc across the entire upper sky. They all questioned each other on what they had wished for, but no one would tell, despite much teasing and guessing.

The evening ended with Mrs. Robey announcing the last dance. Because of their odd number, the three friends spent the last dance out on the porch, leaning on the rail, looking at the stars and listening to "Carolina Moon" played by the orchestra.

The next morning, Kate boarded a bus home for the three-week winter break.

On the ride, she thought about all the things she wanted to tell her family. She imagined them all sitting together, her telling all about her life at school, as when Parke returned home from Honduras. But no. Parke met her at the bus stop in Davenport.

It was so good to see him. Ginger and Baba hugged her hard and even Maggie gave her a quick hug.

She expected things would be the same as before, but they were not. Time had marched on without her presence and she felt as though she was waking from a long sleep. Ginger and Baba cooked in silence. Parke read the paper while Maggie did homework and Kate sat at the kitchen table feeling utterly alone. When they gathered to eat, Baba and Parke asked a few questions.

"How are your studies?" Parke tried.

"Did they do something nice for Thanksgiving? We went to Allen's this year for a change," Baba offered.

"Did you see the new drinking glasses we bought?" Ginger asked.

It was all so banal.

"I have a boyfriend now. His name is Gracen," Maggie announced.

"No, you don't. You're too young," replied Ginger.

Maggie stuck out her tongue at her mother when only Kate was watching. They shared a brief smirk.

The next morning, Kate went out to the barn to see Donabella. The mare perked up at sight of her, nickered, and then blew warm snot all over her sleeve.

"I missed you, too," said Kate, subduing a smile.

Parke followed her shortly. "Hey honey, how are you feeling?"

"Strange. I never thought coming home would feel this way."

They were quiet for a bit. Kate brushed Donabella and Parke sat on a hay bale, smoking.

"I feel the same way whenever I am gone and then return," Parke agreed with his daughter. "When I was away from home at school, when I was in Europe, when I was in Honduras. In your mind, time stops at home when you leave. But it doesn't."

They worked around the barn together in companionable silence for almost an hour. Kate decided she would have to bridge the awkward gap. She went in and asked if she could help make lunch. In the afternoon, she talked Maggie into a walk along the river so her sister could tell her about Gracen. Things gradually felt better after that first day, but her thoughts returned often to her father's words. *Time doesn't stop at home when you leave.*

She visited Mimi and Dottie several times during the break. Mimi talked about Kate growing up and told her that before she knew it she would be starting her own family.

"Mimi! I don't even have a beau."

"Well, one of these days, love will find you. Just make sure it's the real thing before you jump the broom. The best you can hope for is to find a husband that will be your friend. Someone to laugh with and listen to your dreams and worries," her grandmother advised. "This may be hard to believe, but that was how your grandfather was when I met him. He was carefree, confident, kind, smart, and funny. He was an amazing dancer, sweeping me off my feet in the ballroom at the club."

Kate took a long pause, furrowed her brow, and sat forward in the overstuffed chair. "You are surely joking. Grandpa?"

"I am quite serious."

"But what happened? He seemed so unhappy and distance in those years before he died."

"Oh, I know. It was sad to watch," Mimi agreed.

"How does anyone keep that from happening?"

"Well, I will tell you what I think. This life is not much different from going to the movie theater. It is just a longer picture show. So much happens that is beyond our control and we have to work hard to keep our spirits afloat. One thing I have always told myself is that all we really have that is truly ours is our soul. Take good care of your soul and leave the rest to the will of God."

Before long, the break was over and Kate boarded the bus back to Virginia. On settling back in, the girls were all excited to see each other, sharing stories about their time back home. Hattie had a suitor back in Georgia. He was older, twenty-two, and had escaped the draft due to a farming accident that left him with a limp.

"My parents like him and think we might make a good match. He owns property adjacent to my dad's, so it would be of economic benefit to expand the family farm. But I don't know. I like him fine and he is kind and hard working. It's just that he isn't... okay, I'll say it! He isn't Cary Grant. That's the one I am waiting for."

They all laughed. Bridget had been to see *A Connecticut Yankee* on Broadway and had attended several balls in Manhattan during the break. She said the boys in New York were better looking and she expected to find her husband there eventually.

Kate thought about her grandmother's words and silently hoped that all of them found the right man to spend their lives with.

That first Saturday back, she found Hector and Lucas messing around with a small Appaloosa, each trying to stand on her back while the other led her around. It was instantly the best of times and the boys could not stop grinning at Kate, matching her own happy face. Hector told her they had brought something special back from home and told her to plan for an all-day ride the next weekend. She was intrigued.

The afternoon before the big day, she asked the cook if she could have sandwiches packed for a lunch off-campus. She met them at 7:00 a.m. at the stables and they were on the trail shortly thereafter. The boys had scouted an old abandoned road that wound up and around a wooded mountain. The meadow at the top with a large oak tree was the ideal picnic spot. They spread out a blanket and ate the ham and pickle sandwiches Kate had brought. Then, Hector pulled out the surprise: a quart of Tennessee whiskey made right on their family's horse farm. Lucas pulled out two thermoses of sweet tea to mix it with and they poured the liquor in until the thermoses overflowed.

Kate had little experience with alcohol and thought the concoction tasted horrible. After a few sips, though, she started to relax and the boys started getting silly, making her laugh. Though it was January, the sun was warm and, eventually, all three of them fell sound asleep in the meadow. At dusk, Kate woke up shivering, with blurred vision and a throbbing headache. She woke up the boys and they all hurried, as best they could in their impaired condition, to gather the grazing horses and head for the stables.

They arrived after dark to find the stable doors open, all the lights on, and Mr. and Mrs. Robey standing with arms crossed talking to the sheriff. Kate started to shake with fear, dismounted, and vomited on her riding boots. Mr. Robey put the horses up, the sheriff escorted the boys back to their dormitory, and Mrs. Robey walked Kate to the infirmary holding her by the arm.

The next day, she slept and still could not eat by dinnertime. The day after that, her father arrived. She sat beside him in Mrs. Robey's office and listened to her version of the story from the perspective of the person in whose hands Parke had placed his daughter. After what seemed like an eternity, the verdict came in.

"Mr. Lusk, I am sure you understand the position this behavior puts us all in. To be direct, your child is simply too high-spirited for Southern Seminary. I suggest you try Buena Vista School for Girls. It is only twenty miles away and they have a good reputation."

Kate packed her things and hugged her roommates. Elsie and Hattie cried, but Bridget acted superior and disapproving, as if Kate's behavior might tarnish her own reputation.

On the taxi ride to Buena Vista School, Parke reached over and took Kate's hand.

"Is Mom really mad?" she asked.

"She was at first," her father tried to reassure her. "Then, I reminded her of her own antics at your age. Someday, maybe she will tell you about them. We have all suffered through the teen years and done stupid things, but it doesn't mean you're stupid. It's all just part of growing up."

Parke met with the head matron in private, behind closed doors. He secured Kate's admission acceptance and bid her a warm farewell in the front hall of the administration building. It was not nearly as fancy as Southern Seminary and there were no stables. She unpacked in her dorm room, where she would meet her new roommates when classes ended for the day. She would miss Hector and Lucas terribly.

Stepping Stones

KATE FINISHED HER FIRST year at Buena Vista School, named after the town itself. Her classes were more mundane and she felt like she was in training to be a housewife instead of learning how to run a household. Domestic Arts replaced her horsemanship classes and she suffered through sewing and cooking classes. Though her dormitory room accommodated three girls, she only had one roommate due to low enrollment. Betsy Carter's family owned a beach resort on the other side of the state of Virginia. She was down to earth and spent her weekends in comfortable old jeans and saddle shoes just like Kate. They had an easy rapport with each other.

Kate was back home for two months for summer break. Parke suggested she find a temporary job to make a little money before fall semester. She checked at the Pleasant Valley store and the country club, but they did not need any help. She walked along the storefronts in Davenport looking for help wanted signs, but did not find any. Finally, Parke suggested she start coming to work with him. He would give her odd jobs to do and Allen agreed they could pay her thirty cents an hour for up to twenty hours a week. They settled on a schedule of mornings, Monday through Friday. She would ride into town with Parke and then have the afternoons to do as she pleased before riding back home with him.

She started by cleaning the Lusk & Sons office from top to bottom: ceiling fans, windows, washrooms, floors (including under all the desks), and generally removing the buildup of years of tobacco debris and smoke stench. Next, she dug into the piles of papers on every surface and created filing systems. She answered the phone, directed calls, and took messages. She made coffee, washed coffee cups, and went out to pick up lunch for the crew. It was satisfying to serve a purpose and everyone seemed pleased with her presence and her results. In the afternoons, she would walk to the park, take the trolley to the country club, or window shop in town.

She had plans for the money she earned. Ginger was going to help her design and make a short, fully lined tailored jacket with padded shoulders and a longer, pleated, fantail back. Two narrow skirts with flared hemlines would each have multiple coordinating scarves. She spent much time perusing the fabric selection at the five-and-dime store and looking through catalogs of fabrics for special order. In the end, she chose a warm-toned, reddish-gold-brown lightweight worsted wool for the jacket, tan silk for the lining, and deep-dark orange-and-gold patterned rayon-silk blends for the skirts and scarves.

Though she did not really like wearing hats, Ginger talked her into a basic brown, felted wool, shallow crown, narrow-brimmed hat that could be worn as is, or enhanced with fabric, ribbon, or a feather in the future. Kate received her pay weekly on Friday, and Friday afternoon she would buy what she could afford for the next step in the process. They finished the new suit of matching garments just days before her departure for Virginia. She boarded the bus feeling like a completely new person.

When classes resumed, she showed her creations to the Domestic Arts teacher, who gave her extra credit and asked her to show the rest of the girls in the class how it was designed and constructed. The year passed quickly and she finished earning her associates degree. Graduation was in June of 1946. Both Ginger and Parke came by train to witness her graduation ceremony and bring her back to Davenport. Maggie, at fourteen years old, stayed home to help care for Baba whose health had declined over the past year. They warned Kate that she looked different so she would not be shocked. Three days after they arrived back home, Baba died in her sleep. She was fifty-eight years old. They buried her in the Davenport cemetery. Mrs. Zantow, her son Will, their neighbor Dodie, and Mimi joined the family for a brief graveside service. Kate was grateful she had a chance to see Baba before she passed. Kate moved into the old summer kitchen, surrounding herself with her grandmother's few possessions.

Allen agreed, once again, to pay Kate for part-time work for a few months until she found something more permanent. In September, the war finally ended and the country was exuberant. Kate found a job at the soda fountain of the drug store, where she served sandwiches and made milk shakes. She started taking night classes at St. Ambrose University. That fall she completed typing and bookkeeping courses. Her typing class had been all girls, but the bookkeeping class was mixed. Young men asked her out a few times, but she did not take any real interest in her suitors.

She enrolled in business finance for the winter term. The school registrar said that class was for boys, but she dug in her heels and asked her father to vouch for her ability. The school president reluctantly granted permission. She was the only girl in a class with twenty-seven young men, many who had returned home from the war. Among her classmates was Thomas Quinton.

Thomas was of average height and build, putting him level with Kate's five-foot eight-inch stature. He had dazzling blue eyes set in a handsome face and light brown hair that he continued to wear military-style in a crew cut. He had already enlisted in the Army when the U.S. joined the Allies. Stationed in England as a radio and telegraph specialist, he escaped the injuries exhibited by so many other war veterans. He found Kate at the soda counter and reminded her he was in her finance class. She recognized him right away and had instantly been attracted to those beautiful eyes. They started dating regularly and usually spent time together right after her shift ended on Saturday afternoons.

Spending time with Thomas reminded her of the fun times with Hector and Lucas. Thomas took every opportunity to be silly and make people laugh. He was a happy person, a great dancer, and very sexy. His scent of male musk made Kate swoon and she spent much time at the soda shop daydreaming about him. They found new seats near each other in the back row of the night class they shared and passed notes like naughty sixth graders.

He lived with his parents across the river in Rock Island but looked forward to finding a full-time job so he could have his own apartment. His father worked days at the John Deere factory in Moline and usually did not need the car in the evening. Thomas borrowed it for the night classes and sometimes for Saturday night dates with Kate. Other times, they were on foot around town and had to find rides home. It was frustrating for both. They wanted independence and mobility without help from others. That next fall, Thomas found a job doing bookkeeping for an appliance store in Rock Island, walking distance from his parents' home. He brought Kate home for dinner to meet his parents, and she, in turn, invited Thomas to their farm in Pleasant Valley.

Parke and Thomas were cut from the same proverbial cloth. They both liked to tease the girls and play silly pranks. Ginger adored Thomas because he was so much like Parke. After a full year of steady dating, Ginger started making comments about "when you and Thomas are married."

Kate did not mind the idea, but Thomas had never said anything to that effect. They liked spending time kissing and cuddling, but Thomas seemed content with things the way they were. Finally, Kate got tired of waiting and thoroughly seduced him while they were on a picnic in an isolated spot along the river. For better or worse, she conceived that very first time.

Three months later, in September of 1948, she and Thomas sat, hand in hand, in front of Parke and Ginger and told them the news. Well, no one was surprised, really, but the situation did require the planning of a quick wedding before the town gossip mill started up. Parke was building a new garage, with help from his cousin Brent. They put their heads together and revised the design to create a small apartment above the garage for the newlyweds.

Kate and Thomas with both sets of parents and Maggie in tow put on their best clothes and went to the courthouse. There the Justice of the Peace stepped out from behind the counter, ushered them to a nice, large back hallway lined with hanging ferns, and provided a brief ceremony of sorts that he read from a script in a book. Then they went to the hotel, which had the best restaurant in town, to celebrate quietly with a toast to the couple and seafood that had come up on the river that day: shrimp cocktail, linguine with clam sauce, oysters on the half shell, and chilled white wine. Maggie got a shot of wine for the toast. Kate's little sister was excited by all the commotion, and thinking about her own wedding day. She made a secret vow to herself that it would be a lavish affair, not something private at the courthouse.

Thomas and Kate stayed in his childhood room at his parent's house until the apartment was finished in late October. Everyone chipped in to paint the garage and apartment, as well as the main house and barn, in matching red with white trim. The apartment was small but cozy and quaint. Being on the second story gave them a view of the pasture and orchard. Furnishings were pieced together from hand-offs from various sources. They moved in Baba's feather bed and dresser, Dottie gave them an old dropleaf table that had been in her basement, and Kate resurrected two ladder-back chairs from the barn and made new cane seats for them. A wooden countertop was fashioned out of old boards from the pile behind the barn. They had running water for a sink that served both the kitchen and the bathroom; a toilet in a closet-sized space was setup with a small shower. Ginger gave them the boxed-up, old mismatched dishes and silverware from Kate's childhood. In the poor neighborhood of Moline, they found a thrift store and bought secondhand pots and pans, a two-burner electric hot plate, and an icebox. They were saving every penny they made to buy a car.

Earlier that summer, an elderly man was driving an immaculately maintained 1938 Oldsmobile received as a retirement gift from his employer, a very prosperous Chicago industrialist. Before he was aware of what was happening, he suffered a severe brain aneurysm and his car drifted over an embankment and into the Mississippi River. Witnesses reported the location of the sunken car and a tow truck eventually pulled it out of the swift current. The insurance company judged the car to be a total loss and paid the man's widow for her claim. The car landed in a junk yard, where an ambitious young mechanic saw promise in the great metal hulk. He towed it to his shop and cleaned it up from bumper to bumper, including installing new leather seats from another wrecked car. He dropped in a used engine that had not been in the bottom of a river. He listed this refurbished car in the paper with an asking price of $300.00. Thomas was able to negotiate the price down to $275.00, which was all their collective savings from the past year.

Kate was due to deliver in March. She was getting big by January and marveled at how she could go two more months. Ginger gave her advice about what to eat and keeping her feet up to avoid swelling. Kate's employer dismissed her kindly in November when her loose-fitting clothes could no longer hide the truth. She spent time with her mother in the farmhouse kitchen baking, planning, and learning what she needed to know about raising a child. For Christmas, her parents had given her an antique Jenny Lind-style rocking cradle. Ginger had made baby quilts in yellows and blues plus a soft, flannel layette for the newborn.

Maggie had a few friends over one day and they brought a Kodak camera. Maggie stretched out on the hood of the Oldsmobile like a model with her hair in a French roll, wearing red lipstick, and dressed in rolled-up jeans, saddle shoes, and a flouncy low-cut blouse for her portrait. Kate watched from the window feeling like a beached whale.

Thomas was warm and attentive. He embraced her and kissed her goodbye each morning before leaving for work. They shared companionable conversation each evening over dinner and he wrapped an arm around her as they spooned in bed for the night, his hand resting on her belly feeling the movement of their unborn child. Everything felt right and she appreciated the proximity of her parents for her first adventure into the unknown world of parenthood.

When her water broke in the early morning of March 17, they thought they might have a St. Patrick's Day baby. Thomas took her to St. Luke's Hospital, where Kate had been born. Labor contractions came and went for the next twenty-four hours, before she finally gave birth at 10:37 on the morning of the following day.

Thomas, having missed work the day before, had gone in to the office. He received word and rushed to them, holding his baby girl, Victoria Morgan Quinton, in his arms an hour after her birth. She was named after his mother, as well as Ginger's maiden name. Parke, Ginger, Mimi, and Dottie all arrived soon after to marvel at the small, perfect child.

Thomas was an attentive father. He spent evenings and weekends holding her, telling her stories and playing with her when she got a little older. He never shirked the duties of changing diapers or helping with the laundry burden. Kate breast fed for four months and then weened Victoria onto a bottle supplied with fresh goat milk sold right there at the Pleasant Valley store.

It was an exceptionally hot August and Kate sat in the shade with Ginger on the front steps, fanning Victoria who slept in a basinet.

"Mom," she began, "can I ask you a personal question about being married?"

"Sure, what do you want to know?"

"How often do you and daddy make love?"

Ginger laughed. "Is Thomas wearing you out?"

Kate was quiet for a bit and Ginger lost her smile. "Uh, oh. What's wrong?"

Kate pushed the tendrils of sweaty hair off her neck that were escaping from her twisted-up bun.

"I figured that when I was pregnant, he was just afraid of hurting the baby. But, even now, he just doesn't seem interested. I have to force the issue. It doesn't seem natural."

Ginger thought for a minute then said, "You know, I bet you two just need some time away from the baby. Little ones can be all-consuming of your waking—and sleeping—hours. Now that she is on the bottle, you could leave her with me for a weekend and go off camping somewhere. I bet that would do just the trick."

That evening, Kate brought the idea up to Thomas, but he thought it sounded like a lot of extra work. She dropped the subject and they went on with their companionable, if unusual, marriage.

Meanwhile, Maggie turned twenty-one and attracted the attention of a very rich developer from Minneapolis named Matthew Kleinberger who was building a luxury hotel in town. He met her at the country club and found her indifferent, cheeky banter intriguing. He was twenty-eight years old and had inherited the family business that specialized in building and selling commercial properties. The country club extended him a special guest membership for the duration of the construction project.

When Matthew was sixteen, he started working fulltime for his father who told him he did not need a high school degree. He would learn every aspect of the business and become very wealthy at a young age. When the draft rolled around, his father contributed generously to the campaign of a state senator to ensure his son's exemption from the draft.

Maggie would only accept his invitation for a date if they went double with one of her friends, who had a steady boyfriend. The four of them went out twice, once to a movie and once to dinner, before they started dating on their own. Once, he took her by plane to Philadelphia to tour the city and see the Phillies play the Brooklyn Dodgers, where Jackie

Robinson earned the Dodgers a place in the World Series. She was smitten. They dated for only six months before he asked for her hand. Ginger and Parke were shocked at her good fortune and happily agreed to the match.

Matthew's family agreed to pay for the entire wedding because they insisted it would be in Minneapolis and it had to be spectacular. They had six months to prepare. Ginger made Maggie's wedding gown out of white silk satin and handmade lace. It had a square neckline, long sleeves and an eight-foot train. They all drove to Minneapolis, where Parke gave away the bride in an enormous church wedding. The reception was at the Hotel Nicollet with more than 200 guests in attendance. The pile of wrapped presents was enormous. Parke, Ginger, Kate, and Thomas, with eighteen-month-old Victoria, bid the couple goodbye as they boarded a limousine to the airport for their honeymoon in Cuba.

The sharp departure in their relative paths was bothersome to Kate. Though she wished her sister every happiness, the wedding had sealed a rift between them that started long ago. Despite their lack of closeness, they had witnessed each other's lives. They perhaps knew each other better than anyone else could. It was a bittersweet parting.

Mimi was sorry to have missed the wedding but felt the trip would be too much for her. She had recently turned eighty and was feeling her arthritis more each day. Though the insurance money from the house fire had come through long ago, she did not make any effort to find her own place. Dottie's kids were now grown and gone, so she had plenty of space. They were good company for each other while Dottie's husband was at work all day. They had some women friends who came over for lunch and card games, occasionally breaking up the monotony. Dottie's oldest, Millie, also dropped by often.

Allen was spending more time at the Davenport Candy Company. He felt he had earned the time away from Lusk & Sons and was keen to keep learning about the candy business. The Coin brothers, who had started the business, were happy to have his financial expertise and friendship. They were getting ready to retire and had discussed Allen potentially buying the manufacturing operation. At the same time, a large food brokerage business in Des Moines, Richmond Foods, had approached him about acquiring the Lusk & Sons accounts and territory. Allen and Parke deliberated with each other for months. Selling the family business would give Allen enough capital that he could get a bank loan for the remainder. He had detailed profit-and-loss history for the company showing steady gains. The Coin brothers wanted $130,000.00 for their business. Richmond Foods was offering $145,000.00 to buy out Lusk & Sons. This would leave Allen and Parke with $72,500.00 each. Allen negotiated for Richmond Foods to keep on the remaining Lusk & Sons employees, twelve in all.

On an October Tuesday in 1950, Allen and Parke signed the papers to sell out their father's business. One week later, Allen bought Davenport Candy Company and immediately changed the name to Lusk Confectioners. He offered Parke a job there, promising there would no longer be a need for him to travel.

"The accounts are all setup with the big distributors," Allen confirmed. "You would just need to communicate by phone and make sure order deliveries are on time. Ginger would like it that you were home every night of the year."

Parke took two weeks to think it over, explore other options, and talk to Ginger about possibilities. They had a good amount of money from the sale of the family business and needed to make a wise decision that would sustain them for the long term. It certainly was not enough to start the mining operation and Parke had finally realized how risky that would be anyway. He needed a sure bet. Kate and Thomas were included in these conversations. They were not financially stable and Parke worried what would become of them and his grandchild if left behind.

Florida had attracted their attention. It was an up-and-coming state with developers filling-in much of the swampy, mosquito- and alligator-infested property along the coast. Florida was seeking new businesses and offering tax incentives to lure entrepreneurs to its shores. *Business Week* magazine touted Vero Beach as the next Miami and listed the average house price as very affordable. Fast-food franchises were starting to take off across the country. McDonalds and Dairy Queen were making news, with In-N-Out Burger and Carl's Jr. soon to follow the trend. The family speculated that Dairy Queen's soft-serve ice cream would be a perpetual hit in a place where summer lingered on for nine months and people were recreating at the beach. The more they all talked, the more excited they became. Magazines showed palm trees and white-sand beaches with people in bathing suits, straw hats and sunglasses strolling along the boardwalk. All four of them could work at their very own business and not need to worry about income.

Finally, they decided. Parke and Kate agreed to sell Donabella to the country club for $25.00. They knew she would be well cared for there for the remainder of her life. Men came with a horse trailer and loaded her up. Kate shed a few tears but knew it was the right thing to do. Thomas gave notice at his job and they had a yard sale to get rid of everything that would not fit in the two trailers they bought. It was difficult for them to say goodbye to Mimi, knowing they would very likely never see her again. They all promised to write. They sold the house in Pleasant Valley to none other that Will Zantow.

So, the four of them, with little Victoria in the back seat, left in two cars, each pulling a trailer full of belongings to begin a new life in Florida.

Paradise

T HE TRIP TO FLORIDA was full of fun and adventure, largely supplied by Parke and Thomas playing off each other. They left Iowa in the fall when the leaves were turning and the nights were cool. They rotated traveling partners at least once a day and sometimes the girls drove together, with Ginger or Kate at the wheel. They drove south through Illinois, then passed through Kentucky, Tennessee, Alabama, and Georgia. It was a leisurely trip, highlighted by roadside stands selling peaches, apricots, walnuts, and pecans. They stayed at old hotels in small, forgotten towns, and, one night, camped out under the stars in Tennessee to watch a meteor shower. That night, they shared a bottle of Tennessee whiskey sparking passion. Kate and Thomas made stealth love only twenty-feet from her snoring parents. They stopped at diners where locals stared at the foreign travelers and, once, they took a wrong turn down a dirt road and came face-to-face with a Ku Klux Klan guard post at the gateway to a rally. The guards politely pointed them in the correct direction.

Through the Deep South, they saw fields of crops ready for harvest, chain gangs working along the roadways, and spectacular plantation mansions from a bygone era; some were boarded up and in ruins, others were used as old folks' homes, hospitals, or boarding houses. Gas stations were often far apart and on one occasion, they had to syphon gas from one car to the other so they would all make it to the next station. The further they drove, the warmer it became, and they found themselves in summer-like weather once again. The first sighting of a palm tree and, later that day, a citrus grove was a delightful reminder that they were entering what may have well been a new country. Traveling south along route A1 from St. Augustine, they passed through miles of uninhabited jungle. Gradually, little beach towns popped up and signs of new recent development came into view.

When they finally reached Vero Beach after seven days of travel, they rented a suite of adjoining rooms at the Driftwood Inn, steps from the white sand beach. Constructed mostly of actual driftwood, including parts of sunken ships, there was a mast in the front with a bell. That evening, despite their weariness from the drive, they all played in the surf until well after dark, coming back to their rooms with their swimsuits full of sand.

The next day, they walked around town and then drove out in a widening circle to get the lay of the land. Parke arranged for a real estate agent to work with them on finding a suitable location for the new business and a house to buy. The agent was an energetic young man and greeted them dressed in a short-sleeved floral Hawaiian shirt, white cotton trousers, and canvas loafers. He gave them friendly advice where to buy some new clothes fitting of the tropics, which is how they spent the second day.

After that, they divided forces and the men read specifications for the Dairy Queen brand, talked with contractors about designs, and reviewed available commercial sites, both near the beach and near the motor traffic. Meanwhile, Ginger, Kate, and little Victoria went out to look at available homes for sale. They saw several plain, rectangular, cement-block houses with barren sand yards.

"We cannot have a home with no character," Ginger exclaimed. "There must be something better."

At the start of their second week in Vero Beach, something new came on the market. It was only two blocks from the beach, designed by an aspiring architect. It was modern with a high, vaulted central ceiling, an unparalleled set of roof pitches, and was entirely of cypress to withstand the salt air. Windows and fans placed high in the cathedral ceiling captured the sea breeze and circulated it down into the shaded living space. Best of all, a path around the entire house was overhung with trees that shaded the house from the blazing sun and the view of the street. Brilliantly designed, with bedrooms and adjacent bathrooms on either side of the house, it was perfect for their multi-generational household. The kitchen was a small step-up area on one end of the great room, which allowed whoever was cooking to stay involved in the conversation.

Ginger and Kate met the fellas at the hotel restaurant for dinner after a swim in the pool and declared they must see it the following day. Everyone agreed it was a lucky find. They made an offer and closed on the deal after three weeks, the minimum amount of time needed for transfer of deed.

During their stay at the Driftwood, Thomas made friends with the bar manager. He was a very attractive Puerto Rican man, named Luis, about the same age as Thomas. After his shift, he would have drinks with them all by the pool and swim. The time at the beach and pool earned them all healthy, tan, lean bodies.

They arrived with only the bare necessities, so Ginger and Kate's next task was to find furnishings. They visited furniture stores, drove to neighboring towns, strolled through flea markets, and haggled for what they needed. Ginger splurged on having a large, cherrywood table made with leaves that could expand to seat twelve people. She insisted it be taller than normal to accommodate Parke's long legs.

Meanwhile, Thomas and Parke located an ideal location for the new business, literally on the main route between the parking areas and the beach. Construction was underway and the equipment ordered. With plans all set, they had little to do but wait and search for shells on the beach. They had everything they needed and a plan to sustain them into the future. It was a happy time.

Luis offered Thomas a bartending job at the hotel bar to bide the time until he went to work at the Dairy Queen. He said he would teach Thomas everything he needed to know about mixing drinks and serving customers. He readily accepted and began spending evenings there, making remarkably good tips. Luis and Thomas were both so tanned, handsome, and attentive to their customers, that bar sales soared. Guests, especially the young ladies, often asked to have their pictures taken with the two of them.

As the grand opening approached for the very first Vero Beach Dairy Queen, Parke, Ginger and Kate were deep in preparation, learning how to clean and service the equipment, putting out advertising, setting up a bank account, and devising methods for tracking income. It was just days before the grand opening when Thomas told the family he would like to stay on bartending at the Inn. There was a long silence. Then they all started talking at once.

Parke made the point that he would essentially be a part owner of the new business and working there would be like working for himself. Ginger said they needed his bookkeeping skills to keep everything straight. Kate said she was looking forward to the two of them working towards something together.

He was sorry to disappoint them but had made up his mind. He argued that he was making good money bartending and that he really enjoyed the job.

With that decided, Parke, Ginger, and Kate wrote the schedule, sharing all the shifts between the three of them in the short term, with plans to hire extra help eventually. Thomas worked five days a week at the bar and his shift began at 4:00 p.m. It was typical for him to get home after 2:00 in the morning, especially on nights when they had live music. Kate had to concede that the money he deposited into their personal bank account was quite good and he was as attentive as ever to little Victoria, buying her presents frequently. And so, they continued down their odd road of friendship and compatibility, which looked less and less like marriage.

Working at the Dairy Queen turned out to be enjoyable for Kate. It reminded her of the days at the soda fountain, seeing young couples and groups of teenagers out enjoying the hot, endless summer evenings of the beach town. A swamp cooler kept them reasonably comfortable while they worked the sliding window, but Kate sometimes felt sick to her stomach from the heat and humidity.

Parke opened at 10:00 a.m. most days and stayed there through early afternoon until Ginger or Kate took the late shift. They all shared in caring for Victoria. They stayed open until 10:00 p.m. Parke said they could not hire anyone until the three of them knew the business inside and out and had foolproof methods for preventing theft with the all-cash sales. He devised ways to keep close track of inventory and chart daily income to reveal slow days.

The business was an instant hit. It was common to have a line ten people deep at any time of the day or evening. They had ordered the equipment to serve burgers, hot dogs, fries, and soda. But they prudently waited until they had been serving ice cream for a full two months before expanding the menu. Business increased immediately with the addition of food.

It was then that Parke began interviewing additional staff, much to Ginger and Kate's relief. They were all getting tired. He finally hired two young ladies in their early twenties named Sherry and Lois. The new schedule allowed Parke to focus on the books, equipment maintenance, and overall management while still allowing time for his beloved golf. He also made time to write long letters to his mother, who he knew would share them with his siblings, and with Maggie up in Minneapolis.

Ginger and Kate would still each work forty hours each week but did have backup help on food preparation. Ginger thought about all those years that she spent inventing ways to fill idle time. Now she was making money for her family and it felt good.

Three months had passed since their arrival. It was then that Kate knew for sure she was pregnant and already entering her second trimester. Thomas was pleased about expanding their family and Ginger exclaimed that a new baby was a blessing to them all. The days passed quickly, marked by Victoria's growth and the expansion of Kate's girth.

Victoria's sparkling blue eyes and sun-bleached, white-blond locks were enchanting and she entertained them all. She was walking, then running, and talking a blue streak using every word she could possibly pick up from what she heard. The adults all had to be on their best behavior to avoid cuss words or anything they did not want repeated in the grocery store. Thomas watched her in the mornings while Ginger and Kate shopped and ran errands or got ready for work.

Being their own employer—and with the cover of the counter between Kate and the customers—she worked right through her eighth month. Labor pains came quickly after a few weeks of taking things easy at home, and Eliza Jane was born after only six hours. This surprised everyone because this child weighed more than ten pounds. She was chubby, pink, and had a small shock of red hair right on top of her head.

The next two years were a juggling act to keep everything going and take care of the two little ones. They all helped and Kate was grateful to be living with her parents during this time.

Eliza was filled with personality and in need of constant supervision. She tested her world in frightening ways, climbing up high to jump off objects, putting filthy objects in her mouth. One day, she was running too fast and tripped over the edge of the rug, slammed her head on the edge of the coffee table, and required six stitches. She had to go back to the doctor again after she shoved a red crayon so far up her nose none of them could extract it.

Despite these perils, it was a happy time for all of them. They took mini vacations to see more of the beach towns down the coast. They drank gallons of sweet ice tea and lemonade to sustain them through the hottest months and they laughed together at the antics of the children and the funny things they said.

It was just after they celebrated three full years in business, that Parke became ill. First, he simply was often not feeling well and they all attributed it to the heat and his age. He was now sixty years old and a day of golf would completely wear him out. Then, he began losing weight. It was subtle at first, but he never had much body weight to spare. He eventually lost his appetite altogether and Ginger and Kate both insisted he see a doctor.

The routine exam was accompanied by some blood tests that took two weeks to come back. Then Parke had a more thorough exam. The next week, the doctor asked if he could come back and bring his wife this time. There, sitting together opposite the doctor's desk in his back office, they learned that Parke had advanced liver cancer. His prognosis was not good. The doctor simply advised him to get his affairs in order and enjoy every single day he had left. Pain medication would be made available, as well as an appetite enhancer to help him eat when he could.

Kate and Thomas were beside themselves, but Ginger fell apart. She kept vowing she would be strong and then, moments later, would collapse in anguished tears. Parke wrote to his mother, brother, sister, and youngest daughter about the news. He asked that they remember what a great life he had and not to mourn for him. He told his mother he would see her again on the other side. The other side of what he had no clue, but knew it was something his mother would like to hear. He also wrote letters to be sent only after he passed. They were sealed up and given to Kate to mail when the time came.

He taught Kate everything he knew about his role in the business. He told her she had to be the strong one now and see her mother through. It pained Parke to see Ginger and Kate break down sometimes as they talked. He did not want anyone to suffer on his behalf. Parke died two months later at home in his bed after a terrible night, despite the morphine. Thomas helped Kate make arrangements for his burial. They had a graveside service with the immediate family who could afford the trip to Florida: Maggie, Matthew, and Allen.

I N THE MONTHS THAT followed, they thought Ginger would eventually rally and pull herself together, but she slipped further and further into the abyss. She drank herself into oblivion. She could not work. Kate rewrote the schedule and dropped the days they were open from seven to five, with

Mondays and Tuesdays off. Her biggest issue was childcare. Ginger promised again and again to stay sober and watch the girls, but Kate came home to crying children in soaked diapers with no evidence of dinner being made. Ginger would be sound asleep, snoring.

It was during this time that Kate begged Thomas to take some time off to help her. The family was in a crisis and she needed him. In a desperate mood, she went to see him at work one evening when she got off after closing at 10:00. She entered the bar, which was not very busy and, seeing no one behind the bar, went to find him in the back office. She came around the corner and what she saw froze her in her tracks. There was Luis, leaning against the desk with his arms around Thomas's waist. Thomas stood intimately between Luis' spread legs. Thomas's hand was on the back of Luis' head as they locked in a passionate kiss. She could see her husband's erection bulging in his pants. A second after she saw it all, they realized her presence and parted quickly. Neither said a word but stared at her as she looked back and forth between them. She turned and walked out, her entire body shaking with rage, fear, and disgust.

After getting Victoria and Eliza settled into bed for the night, she sat on the front steps smoking a cigarette. She did not smoke often, usually only in social settings after a drink or two. She had to think. Her mother was a total wreck and now, so was her marriage. Maybe it always had been, but now... no, this was different. This was insulting, immoral, and *illegal. Her husband was a faggot, a queer, a homosexual.* She said the words over and over to herself. *How does this happen?* They are married, they have two daughters, and they moved here to start a new and better life. *What was happening?*

She lost her beloved father, her most precious parent, who no matter what had always been there, who always made her feel so loved. She was losing her mother to derangement, depression, and debilitating alcoholism. She had apparently now lost her husband to another person, not a woman, but a man, a very attractive man who any woman would want. But she had not known her husband wanted him. Her husband did not want her. He wanted *him*.

Sitting there, beneath a barren sky, something broke inside her. Something that needed to break so she could escape. It was a barrier, a dam, a closed gateway no longer useful and she needed to blow it to bits. She was no longer a girl in the care of her parents or husband. She was an adult woman with two precious children to care for and it was time to be strong and make difficult decisions. She recalled one of her father's favorite sayings: *Pull yourself up by your bootstraps.*

The first thing she would do was take care of herself and her girls. She went to bed and slept deeply. When she rose, she bathed, put on a favorite yellow sundress and lipstick and dressed Victoria and Eliza in matching red flowered jumpers. She went to the Dairy Queen and hung a sign.

Closed today. Sorry for the inconvenience.

Kate returned home and called Maggie, despite the exorbitant cost of the toll call.

A housekeeper answered the phone and Kate waited for her sister to come on.

"Hello?"

"Maggie, it's me, Kate."

"Kate! Wow. You sound like you are inside a tin can," she laughed.

"Yea, well we are a long way apart. Listen, I need your help. Mom is in a bad way; I am honestly afraid for her life. We need to do something."

"Like what?" Maggie asked.

"I think she needs to go into a mental hospital or something. It's like she has lost her mind and I need help taking care of the kids while I keep the business going. Things are difficult here."

"Well, I am sorry to hear that, Kate, but I can't help. Matthew is traveling a lot for work and he wants me with him. We are very busy. There are new projects underway in Buffalo and Cincinnati. On top of all that, I just discovered I am expecting! Can you believe it? Your little sister is going to have a baby!"

Kate was silent for a few moments. She had not even gotten to the part about her husband. Then she said, unenthusiastically, "Congratulations, sis. I will let you go now. Take care of yourself," and with that she hung up the phone.

She loaded the kids back into the car and drove to the Indian River County Courthouse where she filed for a divorce. She cited "irreconcilable differences." Her next stop was at the Department of Children's Services. She explained that her father had just died and she was going through a divorce. Her mother was the primary source of childcare for her daughter and her mother was unfit. She explained that she had a business to run and would probably need to have her mother put into a treatment center. She asked if Children's Services could help her.

"Mrs. Quinton, if you stay home with your children, there are services we can offer. But if you choose to work fulltime, we can only offer the support of foster care for your girls."

The woman stared at her, waiting. Kate thought for a long moment. She knew she could never attain anything better for herself and her daughters if she relied on welfare. It would only keep them alive and little else. Her plan was to open her own bank account and not touch one penny that her husband had earned. She wanted nothing from him ever again.

In a bitter exchange that would haunt her forever, she signed the papers to have her children put into foster care. She insisted repeatedly to the woman behind the desk that this was only temporary.

The woman pursed her lips and said, "Of course. As you wish."

Clearly, this was unorthodox. Children were *taken* by Children's Services, not deposited with them. Arrangements were made for Victoria and Eliza to be brought back the next day with their clothing and favorite toys. At two and four years old, neither understood the magnitude of what was about to happen.

When they returned home, Ginger was awake and belligerent. She hurled epithets at them from which Kate wanted to protect her children. She packed all her husband's clothes into boxes, folding them neatly as she always had. She put Victoria and Eliza in the car with her and drove to Luis' house. It was evening by then, so she knew Thomas and Luis were both at the bar. She left everything on the front porch. On the way home in the car, little Victoria repeated Ginger's words, calling Kate a whore. Kate decided the best thing to do was to ignore it and make sure her child was better sheltered from there forward. She went home and packed two small suitcases, one for each child. She tucked in two favorite toys for each and hoped their placement would be in a home with other children and plenty of toys for all.

"Where are we going, mommy?" asked Victoria.

"You are going on an adventure, to meet new people, and sleep over at a new place."

"We are moving to a new place?"

"No, honey. You will stay at a new place and I will come see you every few days. You will be well cared for and have fun playing with other children, while mommy takes care of other things. Sound okay?"

Victoria stared at the floor, deep in thought, trying to understand.

That night, Victoria and Eliza slept in Kate's bed snuggled in close holding their teddy bears.

Everything is going to be okay, Kate told herself. *I am doing what I need to do to take care of my children and myself and to eventually make everything better.*

The next morning, she made bacon and waffles, dripping with butter and maple syrup, for the kids. It was their favorite. They then went in the car to the Children's Services office. They walked, Kate holding both of their hands, which she placed into the hands of a social worker.

She got down on one knee, level with their little faces, and said in a voice she hoped sounded cheerful, "Be good girls and have fun. I will see you in a few days."

Kate kissed them each on the forehead, turned, and walked out the door. When she got to the car she broke down, hyperventilating and crying all the way home, the streets swimming in front of her. At noon, she met both Sherry and Lois at the Dairy Queen, took down the closed sign, and put the daily change into the cash drawer. She gave them each a new schedule for the coming two weeks and left them to work the rest of the day. She then went to the courthouse and requested a hearing with a judge.

She sat in the waiting area outside the courtroom for hours as people came and went before the judge. Finally, at 3:30 p.m., a clerk escorted her to the judge's inner chamber. There, she told the elderly, white-haired judge about her mother. She explained the recent death of her father and that she had seen this behavior before. She said that she thought committing her mother could be the only way to save her life. The judge listened carefully, asked questions, and was thoughtful.

He said that he would order a doctor from the sanitarium to assess her mother and, if warranted, order transport to Orlando for admittance and treatment. The doctor came five days later. He sat on a chair in Ginger's room while she laid in bed with the covers over her head. She had not eaten in days. The only thing she said was that she wanted to die. Later that day, two men came and got her up out of bed. They put her in a straightjacket and placed her in the back of a car with a screen between the front and back seats. Kate watched them drive away and wondered if she would ever see her mother again alive.

Loose Tethers

K ATE'S VISITS WITH VICTORIA and Eliza were on Wednesday evenings and Sunday afternoons. It was a blessing they were placed in the same home together. Because of the unusual circumstances of their relinquishment, rather than seizure, Children's Services allowed Kate to take them out for visits. She picked them up at a large house where she saw at least three other small children playing. Sometimes, she took her girls out for a picnic and sometimes they went to the beach or park to play together. Victoria and Eliza seemed to be doing okay. They got used to the routine and grew confident their mother would always come back. The resilience of children is a wonder.

All the rest of Kate's time was spent working. She only took time off to see the kids. She scheduled Sherry and Lois to help her during busy hours, but she worked solo as much as possible to save on wages. She opened a bank account in her own name and carefully tracked her time to prove she withdrew only fair wages from the business account. She compared inventory to cash sales every day to make sure there was no waste and no missing money. At night, she fell into bed and slept a dreamless, deathlike sleep, occasionally woken by the phone ringing at all hours. She knew it was Thomas and refused to answer. He also knocked at the door a few times early in the day before work. She kept the front and back door locked.

After about a month, she received a letter from an attorney. Thomas was contesting the divorce insisting on compensation for his share of the car and visitation rights with is daughters. The next day, Kate asked Lois and Sherry to cover for her at work and she went straight to that attorney's office. She did not have an appointment and sat stoically for two hours in the waiting room.

When she was finally admitted and offered a seat across from him, she said directly and flatly, "Your client, Thomas Quinton, is a sodomite. Correct me if I am wrong that the state of Florida classifies this as unnatural and lascivious, punishable by fines and imprisonment. I have not told a single person about his relationship and cohabitation with his queer lover, but if you drag me into court, I will most certainly apprise the judge of the truth. I suggest you advise your client accordingly."

With this, she stood up, straightened her skirt, leveled him a scathing look, and marched out of the office. She did not hear from Thomas or his attorney again.

It was three months later that she received a letter written in her mother's own hand. She told Kate she was about to be released. She also said that she would never forgive her daughter for putting her in that place. They had subjected her to shock therapy and strange mind-altering medications. She told Kate to find a new place to live, that she did not want to see her.

This was what Kate expected and she was ready. She laid out all the financial records for the business, as well as a two-week schedule for Lois and Sherry to cover entirely on their own in case Ginger refused to work. After that, it would all be up to her mother to figure out. Kate had saved enough money to rent her own place. She found a small beach cottage directly adjacent to the sand beach on the other end of town. She would be gone by the time her mother arrived. She packed her things, moved into her new home, and went to get her children. She would start applying for jobs immediately and use her savings to secure daycare for Victoria and Eliza. She had made it through this horrible time as best she could and would rebuild her life.

Kate had found a new job within a few weeks after moving to the cottage. She stretched the truth a bit, reasoning that necessity was the mother of invention, and told prospective employers she had worked extensively in her father's food brokerage business since she was sixteen, before owning her own business, which she lost in a divorce.

These fabrications, along with her presentation of a mature and serious manner, won her a fulltime secretarial job at a Federal Fish Hatchery at Indian River Shores just on the outskirts of town. She spent her weekdays there doing standard secretarial work: answering and directing phone calls, typing correspondence dictated by the director, filing paperwork, filling out government reports, ordering supplies, running to the post office to send outgoing mail, bringing back incoming mail from the regional office in Atlanta, and cleaning up messes the men did not even see.

Kate and her girls loved the beach cottage. The back steps were directly on the sand beach and they spent their time together in swimsuits, playing on the beach and in the surf. Kate found a seventeen-year-old neighbor, Allie, who gladly watched the girls there at home when Kate was at work. Allie was saving to go to nursing school and she accepted all the hours Kate would give her. She doted on the girls, prepared them good, nutritious meals, and made sure their naps lasted at least two hours every day.

It was three months after Ginger's return home from the asylum before she contacted Kate. She called to ask if she could see the girls and told Kate she had something for her. Kate said she could come by the cottage on the weekend. After all, it was not Kate that severed their ties, but her angry mother. Kate hoped this outreach meant Ginger was feeling ready to reconcile.

Her mother arrived on a Saturday afternoon, to the delight of the girls. They had spent much time with their "Granny Ginge" and their bond was close. Things were a bit awkward between Kate and her mother, but it was at least civil and now, they had the opportunity to mend.

Remembering Parke's request that she help take care of her mother after he was gone, Kate was relieved to pull this loose family tether back in close where it belonged.

After greeting the girls with tons of hugs and kisses and catching up on all their chitter chatter, Ginger handed Kate a sealed envelope addressed to her in her father's hand.

"I found this recently when I cleaned out your father's study." Ginger tried to smile.

Apparently, he had included her in his letter writing and knew it would surface after his death. Kate tucked it into an apron pocket while she fixed lunch for them all.

At the end of the visit, Kate gave her mother a brief hug, hardly reciprocated. *That's okay*, Kate thought. *Take your time.*

That night, after the kids were sound asleep and she was relaxing with a glass of cool wine and listening to the surf, she carefully opened the letter.

Dearest Kate, my precious firstborn child,

I never dreamed I could love someone so much that I would lay down my life to protect them until the day I met you. The value of your presence in my life was immeasurable. As I contemplate the end of my life on earth, I am filled with gratitude for the gifts you gave me. I remember you as a small child, so serious and forthright. I remember you as a growing child, inquisitive, quick to learn, and surprisingly opinionated. I remember you as a young woman riding trails with me for hours, telling me about your thoughts and dreams. I remember you as an adult full of business sense and work ethic.

We do not have the honor of knowing what lies beyond death. But if there is any way that I can see you and witness your life, I will be nearby. I will be there in the gentle breeze, the shape of a cloud, the colorful sunset, and in your dreams. I will always remember you and love you more than anyone else on earth can. You will always be loved.

Your Father

Kate read the letter three times and wept. The letter became the most precious thing she ever owned.

After that first icebreaker visit from Ginger, she started seeing her on a regular basis, tentatively at first, and then as a standard weekend commitment. Sometimes, Kate dropped the girls off at Ginger's house before going out shopping. Ginger was definitely never drinking again after her horrific time while institutionalized.

Eventually, Kate asked about the Dairy Queen. They talked a little here and there about it and Kate figured out she had delegated just about everything to employees. Sherry had quit to get married. Lois was still there, along with three new employees. Ginger said business had dropped off lately. She said she did not know why but claimed she was making enough for what she needed, which was not much. Her house mortgage was paid. She just needed enough to pay the water, electric, and phone bills, and to buy her groceries.

Kate did not believe for one minute that business was down. She saw that Ginger was not running the business carefully and employees were likely taking advantage. She offered to look over the books to see if she could detect any patterns regarding the declining revenues. Ginger declined.

"No, it's okay. You are busy enough with work and the kids. I will take care of the Dairy Queen."

So, Kate backed off. She and her mother were not close, but they shared an intense love for Victoria and Eliza. Where the children were concerned, they would confer at length over best practices and strategies regarding behavior, manners, nightmares, refusal of vegetables, and the like. Beyond that, they were distant, which did not particularly disturb Kate. After all, she and her mother had never been close.

She thought often of her grandmother Mimi's wise words and worked hard to keep her mind clear of distractions and burdensome fears. She focused her sights on peace, contentment, and joy. But, out of curiosity, she strolled by the Dairy Queen one afternoon. To her surprise and horror there was a new sign that read:

Blacks served only when there are no whites present. No exceptions.

She went straight to her mother's house and confronted her. "Mother! How can you hang that sign?! You want to chase off half the customers?"

Ginger was smug. "No, I want to keep customers. I saw black people sit right there at the picnic table while white folks were standing around eating. It was disgraceful."

"So what? What about all your talk about loving the 'Nigras' back in Mississippi?"

"In Mississippi, they knew their place. They stayed in their own part of town and there was not any trouble. These black people here walk down the street like they own it."

"Daddy would be so upset to hear you talk like this," Kate shot back.

"Well, this was something we never agreed on," Ginger declared.

After this, Kate did not walk near the Dairy Queen. It bothered Kate horribly when she realized that her mother was undoubtedly teaching her children prejudice. Kate would just have to *unteach* it. It would be wrong to deny Ginger access to the girls. They all adored each other.

Occasionally, Kate would ask Ginger to care for the children in the evening so she could go on a date. Ginger was always agreeable but also cautioned Kate about bringing another man into her life.

"You have to put the children's needs first, not your own," she said.

This chaffed at Kate, but she refused to engage in conversation with her mother about it. Who was Ginger to give Kate advice? The truth was that she really did not want a man in her life. Her acceptance of dates was just for a change of pace. A night out for dinner, dancing, or a movie was sometimes fun, if the right man asked. But she allowed them only a brief goodnight kiss on the cheek and no more. She had a few second dates but refused third dates.

She had worked hard and sacrificed much to attain independence and freedom. She did not need to cater to anyone else's needs, listen to their counsel, or consider their happiness above her own and her children's happiness. She thought that someday it might be possible to find a true companion, someone who only wanted to be her best friend and who would love her for the sheer joy of sharing a life together.

Ginger hired a gardener. Kate figured her mother must have determined what was draining her income to be able to afford such a luxury. Ray was an older man with a tall, thin frame and a kind face. He was there every time Kate dropped off or picked up the kids. How was her mother affording this?

Then, one day, she followed Ray into her mother's house to get something cold to drink in the kitchen. He went to the back hallway. She assumed he was using the bathroom, but after twenty minutes he did not reappear. She tiptoed down the hall to the room she and Thomas used to share. The door was open and there she saw Ray laying on the bed, taking an afternoon nap. She could clearly see his clothes hanging in the closet and strewn on the dresser, along with a shaving cream mug and razor. He was living there!

This revelation was intriguing. She did not mention it to her mother but went home to think about it. It was clearly unorthodox for a widow to live with a man to whom she was not married. On the other hand, she did not want her mother to be lonely. Kate also really liked Ray. He was kind, gentle, and sincere.

They all continued to avoid discussion of the obvious situation and Ginger introduced Ray to everyone as her gardener. Kate wondered if they were in love or just friends. She wondered if they ever slept together. In the end, she decided none of it mattered. Ginger was doing what Mimi would have done: letting life unfold unfettered by social conventions. Kate was happy for her.

Kate started taking more time to really notice her surroundings and live in the moment. She admired the cloud formations, the beautiful sunrise, and the butterfly that landed on her arm, pointing them all out to her children. She decided that, whether actual or imagined, she would consider perfect moments a gift from her father, a touch point between souls. She also made a commitment to nurture flying dreams in her children. With this new view of life, the sky no longer seemed barren but full of light and hope.

Winter Love

I N OCTOBER, GINGER RECEIVED a letter from Maggie. She had given birth to a precious baby boy named Jeffrey, unfortunately diagnosed with the dreaded hemophilia curse. It was a terrible blow and it would deeply affect Maggie's life as she strove to provide some quality of life for her son. No sports, no playing in the woods or tree climbing, no exposure to biting flies. It was a terrible prognosis. Ginger told Kate the news and Kate truly felt sad for her sister. It made her feel blessed for her two healthy children and made her fearful of having any more.

Ray helped Ginger with some deep cleaning and debris removal that month. Neither one cared for routine house cleaning, though both had hobby projects going everywhere. Ginger liked to knit, crochet, sew, do needlepoint, and make braided rugs from wool scraps. Ray, in addition to obsessive flower gardening, enjoyed making miniature dollhouse furniture and garden benches. They sold their wares on weekends at the flea market. The house was always a mess of half-finished projects and a thick layer of dust. In this regard, they were perfect companions. Ginger embroidered a sign that hung in the hallway:

A clean house is the sign of an empty mind.

During this long-overdue cleaning spree, Ginger discovered a box of papers related to the mines in Honduras. She had put all that out of her mind long ago and when she next saw Kate, gave her the box.

"Do whatever you want with it. I think it is worthless," she said.

In the evenings after the children were sound asleep, Kate took time going through it all. In addition to the correspondence with Hawkins, she found detailed legal descriptions her father had obtained from the Department of Mines in Tegucigalpa. More intriguing were the financial projections Parke and Allen had put together, showing the needed capital and expected returns over time. She then decided to replicate their spreadsheet using current information that she would seek to obtain. She told her employer she needed an afternoon off for a personal matter and set up a meeting with the president of Farmers Bank and Trust Company.

Mr. Chapman was a rotund man in his fifties and dressed in a suit and tie that looked too tight and very hot for the climate. Kate explained that she had some extra money from an inheritance and wanted his advice about whether gold and silver would be good investments at this time. Oozing false charm, Mr. Chapman clearly believed that Kate was asking him to buy gold for her.

"Madam, you are obviously a very discerning investor. Gold would be an excellent place for you to appreciate the value of your holdings over time," the banker advised.

Kate smiled, "Yes, of course, but do you think it is the *best* investment at this time?"

"Oh, yes!" he assured her. "I will be happy to arrange everything for you."

Kate was getting annoyed. "Can you tell me how the value of gold today compares with five years ago? And are there predictions for its value rising or falling in the coming years?"

"My dear Mrs. Quinton, the beautiful thing is that you can leave all this to Wall Street and simply enjoy knowing your money is safe." He gave her a smarmy smile dripping with self-interest.

"Thank you, Mr. Chapman. I will see myself out. I do hope you enjoy the rest of your day." Kate left as quickly as she could before he could catch her. *What a waste of time.* She could see she was not on the right path yet. After a few days of thinking it over, she wrote a letter to Maggie.

October 13, 1956

Dear Maggie,

Mother told me about your son's diagnosis. I am so very sorry. My heart goes out to you. I look forward to a day soon when we can see each other and I can hold little Jeffrey in my arms. I know mother would also love to see you both. I hope you will think about a trip here to Florida.

I have been spending time going through Daddy's papers and wonder if I might impose on Matthew to look some things over. There was an investment idea Daddy was working on and I have a notion that Matthew's legal team would be able to assess its merit, or lack thereof. The box is large and will be costly to ship,

but I can write a synopsis and only send the most critical pieces
if he is interested. It could potentially benefit all of us.

Please write back and let me know how you are and what
Matthew thinks about reviewing the papers.

Love, Kate

Victoria had started kindergarten that fall, so Allie only had Eliza during the day. This cost Kate less money, but also meant Allie was not earning enough. She asked if she could bring another little girl, Mae, who was Eliza's age, over during the day, so her pay stayed the same and Eliza had someone to play with. Kate agreed and they continued with their routine. Every afternoon at 3:00, Allie, Eliza, and Mae walked to the main road to meet Victoria when she got off the school bus. Sometimes, Victoria fell sound asleep on the bus and the bus driver had to wake her up at her stop.

There was a new employee at the fish hatchery named Bret. He had been working as a student teacher and trying to decide on a thesis topic for his master's degree, when a temporary job opened at the hatchery. It seemed a logical next step for his biology studies and could provide some practical experience to add to his résumé. He was twenty-five and prematurely bald. He had a quiet, calm demeanor, and stood in the office talking with Kate with his thumbs tucked in the lower edge of his pants pockets. He talked with her about his background, growing up in Dallas, Texas, joining the Navy at only seventeen years old when Pearl Harbor was attacked (his parents had to give permission), and going to college at Oklahoma State A&M. He found the job opportunity on a board in the guidance counseling office.

A one-room apartment onsite came with the job and he was stuck there without a car. Occasionally, he asked Kate for a ride to town after work to pick up groceries. He would catch a local bus back. Kate knew he was not making much money because she processed his pay requisitions. He finally found the courage and said he would like to take her out.

Out of consideration for his financial situation, Kate suggested a beach picnic that weekend. She dropped the kids off at Ginger's for the afternoon and picked him up in her car. They went to one of the nicer white sand beaches, found a place in the shade for their blanket, and he opened his satchel to reveal a picnic of crusty French bread from the bakery, cheese, fruit, nuts, and pop. They had a lovely afternoon swimming, snacking, talking, and walking along the beach looking for interesting driftwood and seashells.

The following week, he asked if she would like to do it again. She agreed and offered to bring the picnic this time. She brought cold fried chicken, twenty-four-hour salad—a favorite made from fruit and marshmallows—and Hershey chocolate bars. They told stories and laughed. He talked more about his parents who were both high school teachers with bachelor degrees. Kate was impressed that his mother had a college degree and thought they must be a very fine family. She wondered what her mother would think about Bret.

Their third date just happened, neither planned nor agreed to. Kate was getting off work and Bret was still hanging around the grounds taking care of a few things, when a bird hit the window startling them both. They went to see what it was only to find an egret, dazed and confused, staggering around. Bret said it was a miracle its neck was not broken. They found a cardboard box, wrapped the bird in a towel, and placed it gently in the box to recover. After, they sat in the office talking quietly while occasionally looking in on the wide-eyed bird.

Kate called Allie, who agreed to make the girls dinner and give them baths. While they sat, Bret shared stories about his many wildlife rescue adventures at summer camp in Wisconsin where his father taught each summer. He learned to fish, hunt, and live in the wilderness over and over again, each summer, until it was all second nature. Soon, he was old enough to be a camp counselor there himself. He also had a big heart for wildlife preservation and raised a fawn one summer, baby rabbits the next, and a nest of baby crows the following year. Kate was impressed with his generous heart.

After two hours flew past, Bret determined that the egret was ready for release. They took the box outside, opened the lid, and gently placed the egret on the grass. The bird sat for a moment letting its eyes adjust to the light. Then it looked at each of them, turned away, and lifted off to sail into the jungle. It was heart-warming, intimate moment.

Two weeks later, Bret asked Kate if she would like to hike into the jungle with him to document butterfly species. He was still exploring ideas for his thesis and wanted to collect some preliminary data for this idea. Despite her rule about no third dates, she reasoned that this was not so much a date as an opportunity to get some exercise and look for butterflies. She agreed and, once again, they had a great time together.

Bret received his paycheck the next week and asked her out to dinner at an Italian restaurant. They had a comfortable, easy rapport and she agreed, reasoning that they were just good friends. They had wine with dinner, which went straight to their heads since neither had much experience drinking. That night, Bret drove Kate home in her car. The kids were sound asleep and Kate sent Allie home. Bret and Kate sat out on the back porch facing the surf and stayed up past midnight. Bret gave Kate a goodnight kiss, brief but on the lips, and drove himself home in her car. The next day was Sunday and he came back at noon. He met the girls and spent the day showing them interesting things in their environment: bugs, fish bones, and a crab on the beach. He made a beach fire where they cooked hotdogs on sticks he whittled. That night, Kate and Bret slept together.

Kate woke up at 4:00 a.m. deeply conflicted. He was a kind, considerate lover—and she was a willing participant in what had happened—but this was not where she planned their friendship to go. Now, they were due at work at 8:00 and she needed to protect her reputation. She gently woke him and asked him to get dressed. She said she needed to get him home. He reluctantly got up, dressed, speaking with her in whispers so as not to wake the children, and got in the car. Kate left the children home alone while she drove Bret back to his lodgings. He leaned over for a kiss and she gave him just a quick peck on the cheek.

That day at work, it was awkward between them. Kate focused on her job and attending to the needs of her boss. She did not even make eye contact with Bret. The following day, she arrived early before any other staff and Bret was already preparing feed for the fish. He stopped what he was doing, washed his hands, and followed her into the office.

"Are you alright?" he asked.

"Hi Bret," she spoke softly. "I am so sorry I could not talk with you yesterday. I am trying to sort out how I feel."

"Okay. I understand. Did I do something wrong? Do you think we made a mistake?"

"You did not do anything wrong. I don't want you to feel that way."

They were quiet for a moment. Kate's instinct was to dive into her work and ignore him, but that would be wrong. She needed to attend to this.

"Bret, I am so sorry. You are so sweet and we have a lot of fun together. I have really had a good time with you this winter. In fact, you have made it special. But I am not seeking a long-term relationship."

Bret thought about this. Then he said, "I can understand that you went through a divorce and you are scared, but I think we have a really good thing going. I want you to know that I will not hurt you. If you give me a chance, I would take care of you and your children. We could be happy together."

Kate sat very quietly for several moments and gazed out the window. Then, she saw the director's car pulling in. "We can talk later, okay? I need to get to work."

With this, Bret left her office and went back to his tasks. He was nowhere in sight when she left for the day and she was grateful. She needed to think. Before the kids went to bed, they asked about Bret.

"Is he your boyfriend, mommy?" asked Victoria.

"No, honey. We are just good friends."

"It was fun cooking hot dogs," said Victoria.

"Yea," said Eliza. "He was nice."

That evening, she sat alone on her back porch, listening to the surf. Life could be lonely sometimes, but she was doing fine. She was putting her children's needs first—along with her own. She had not intended to become intimate with Bret. It just happened. They were human. He was a great guy, but that was no reason to change the path of her life. She did not need a husband. Her mind wandered off into "what if" territory.

Was she preventing her children from having a normal life? Did they need two parents? Was she not considering their needs by denying them a father? What would Mimi say?

That night, Kate dreamed she had to choose a husband. Her choices were Thomas, who appeared in her dream with Luis, her cousin Bob, Mr. Chapman at the bank, or Bret. She woke up with her heart pounding, feeling backed into a corner. It was an intensely uncomfortable feeling. She knew she had to dig deeper to get to her true feelings.

The next day she left work, determined to take some extra time for herself. She knew the girls were in Allie's competent hands and would appreciate the extra money for working a bit later than usual. Kate drove to the old military training grounds where the Brooklyn Dodgers came for off-season practice. Though it was not yet spring, some of the team had come early to get a head start. She sat in the stands, lit a cigarette, and watched the men practice playing a game she knew little about. She appreciated their athletic physiques, fast movements, commitment to the game, and competitiveness. She thought about how men played games like this because they could no longer do hand-to-hand combat to protect their family, their home, their village. What else were they supposed to do with all that pent up anger? Sitting idle was like testosterone poisoning.

The infamous Jackie Robinson was there that evening. Watching him smash the ball over the fence, again and again, was awe inspiring. Some miscreant teenagers loafed around the edges of the field shouting, "nigga, nigga, nigga," whenever Jackie was focused on a play. The players seemed oblivious, ignoring the youths, until one of them threw a rock in Jackie's direction. The manager turned on his heels and marched toward them, sending the kids running like scattered rats.

As she sat, she could feel someone approaching her from the side. She did not look. She did not want company or the obligation to exchange pleasantries. The person came within ten feet of her, an obvious violation of her personal space in the bleachers that only had a dozen people present. Finally, it was unavoidable and she looked up, then over. It was Thomas.

"Kate," he said softly, nothing more. Moments passed. "Can I sit and talk with you for a minute."

Kate hesitated then gestured slightly with a glance at the seat beside her for him to sit. They sat side by side with two feet between them for about five minutes.

Finally, Thomas said, "Kate. I am sorry I hurt you. I know you don't understand what I am or why I love Luis. But I do. I love him. I also love you."

Kate reacted and began to speak, but Thomas stopped her.

"No. Please... just wait and listen." He sighed and looked away. "I love you and I love the children we brought into the world together. I love them with all my being. I am sorry I have hurt you. I am sorry I am not the man you thought I was, but I am not a bad person. I am a kind and loving person. You know that. You know me. I am not a monster."

They sat still again for another five minutes. Kate thought about how much fun they once had. He was her best friend and she missed him. She took time to contain her anger before she spoke. Finally, Kate turned to him and said, "I believe you. I believe you cannot help who you are. I believe you love your children. But I cannot expose them to your lifestyle. It is not wholesome, or moral, or legal. It is an abomination."

"I am sorry you feel that way. I care for you deeply. I love Luis. I want to spend the rest of my life with him."

"Then just sign the divorce papers," Kate said.

"I will. I just wish you would not hate me."

They sat in silence again. Eventually, she turned to him and said, "I don't hate you. I feel sorry for you. Do you know how much misery you will bring down on yourself? People do not accept this. You will be harassed the rest of your life."

"So be it. I can't change who I am or who I love. My last wish is that when the girls get older, you will tell them about me and let them find me if they want to. Please don't tell them I am bad. Let them decide on their own."

He stood up and walked away. Her heart pounded in her chest as she realized she would very likely never see him again. Signed divorce papers arrived in the mail two weeks later.

She had been avoiding Bret during this time, but now he was almost finished with his temporary assignment and would soon be leaving for Oklahoma. He came to see her at the cottage, unannounced on a Saturday morning.

She was standing at the stove, boiling eggs and frying bacon for egg salad sandwiches with bacon bits for lunch. He knocked on the front door and then stepped in when he caught her eye. The girls were playing on the back porch. They stopped playing to eavesdrop on the conversation.

"Kate, I am so happy when I am with you," he started. "I don't want to say goodbye. I am supposed to leave for school in two weeks. We need to talk."

After a quick glance back at her cooking, she said, "Bret. I am glad you came by. We do need to talk. Listen, let me finish making lunch and then we can take a walk after the girls lay down for their naps. Okay?"

"Okay," he said. "Can I help?"

"Sure," she smiled at him. "How about getting some lettuce out of the ice box and washing it?"

They all ate lunch together. Kate read the girls a story while they settled down for a nap. When they were asleep, Kate and Bret walked down toward the water's edge where they had privacy and were out of earshot in case the girls were faking sleep.

Bret took her hand and said, "Kate, I really think we have something here. I don't want to just walk away. Would you consider coming with me? I would be there for you and the girls... we could be happy together. I don't need to finish school. I could apply for more Fish and Wildlife Department jobs, start my career."

Kate smiled at him. "You are a sweet man and I have so much enjoyed our time together, Bret, but I don't really want to get married again. And I definitely don't want any more children. Not because I don't love children, but because hemophilia runs in my family. You know what that is, right?"

He nodded his head, wide eyed. She waited for it to sink in. "The risk of bearing a male child and having him cursed with that sickness is not something I can do. But you... you deserve to have your own children. You have to go forward and follow your path."

Bret was quiet. It was not what he wanted to hear, but he had to respect her feelings. That afternoon, they said a bittersweet goodbye.

Over the next six weeks, Kate worried herself sick that her period was late. Bret had used a condom, but she knew they were not foolproof. She was the fool. How could she have let this happen? She started imagining writing the letter to his forwarding address in Stillwater, Oklahoma. He would be elated and the course of her life would be set. Then, finally, it came, staining her favorite white linen pants and she was never so relieved. Her intense stress and anxiety were likely the reasons for her abnormal cycle. She laughed at herself for falling prey to her own racing brain. Bleach saved the pants and luck saved Kate.

———❀———

Faith

J UST BEFORE CHRISTMAS, DOTTIE called Ginger to tell
her that Mimi had passed quietly in her sleep. She was
eighty-four and had been suffering from undiagnosed aches
and pains for the past five years. It was a blessing given her
discomfort. Ginger called Kate to let her know. Kate said a
special prayer for the peaceful rest of her grandmother's soul.
She did not tell her children the news, but she grieved that
they did not have the opportunity to know her. She was a very
special person with a deep understanding and reverence for
life.

Kate received a Christmas card from Maggie in mid-January,
apologizing for not being in touch sooner. She wrote, "You cannot imagine how much work a newborn is." Kate appreciated
the deadpan humor, but wondered how things were truly going
for her sister. There was no mention of Matthew's being willing
to look at the papers about Honduras.

Kate decided to re-review everything and write up a synopsis
anyway, thinking it would come in handy at some point. She
went to the Vero Beach Public Library and asked about business
magazines.

"I am sorry, miss, but we do not subscribe to any such publications," the senior librarian told her. "However, *Nation's Business Magazine* is available at the University Library in Gainesville. I can order them on interlibrary loan if you would like."

The four most recent issues were available for her to review the following week, greatly enhancing her projections with current information.

Then, much to her surprise, she received a letter from Matthew on Kleinberg Development Corporation stationery, undoubtedly typed up by his secretary.

February 2, 1957

Dear Kate,

Maggie spoke with me some time ago about a business interest you wanted to share with me. I apologize for the long delay in getting back to you. My development business has taken flight in the past year and we are enjoying a record number of big projects in four different states. To meet this challenge, I have tripled my staff, including the addition of three attorneys to handle the nuances of business across state borders.

I would welcome information about the idea you are working on. My team is well suited to discern its worth. Please send what you have directly to my attention here at the office and I promise to follow up on it.

Best wishes to you, your children, and your mother,

Matthew Kleinberg CEO

He signed the letter "Matt" in blue ink. The very next day, Kate stayed late at work to type up her ten-page proposal, which she put in the mail to Matthew the next day. Two months later, Matt sent her a second letter asking if she could come to Minneapolis. He would buy her a plane ticket. She was so excited she could hardly contain herself.

She arranged for Ginger and Allie to share the childcare duties. There was no way her boss would understand the truth about her trip. As his secretary, she had a duty to him and her job. She invented an elaborate family emergency having to do with her sister's child, but promised it would only be for a few days. This fabrication made her feel immensely guilty, but she could not think of another way.

It was thrilling to board a Pan Am flight in Orlando. They stopped in Chicago and then went on to Minneapolis, where the family chauffeur met her at the gate holding a sign that read: "Katherine Lusk." Kate appreciated her sister's use of her given name.

Maggie's home was grand, with a circular drive, massive front door, and a central atrium with a chandelier and sweeping staircase. A servant showed her to her room, which was bigger than her cottage in Vero Beach.

That first night, Maggie and Kate stayed up until 1:00 in the morning, talking about adult life. It was the best time they ever had together. Little Jeffrey woke up during the night and Kate offered to care for him, leaving Maggie to rest. He was so precious and seemingly perfect in every way, unless you knew how fragile he was.

The following afternoon, the chauffeur took Kate downtown to Matthew's twelve-story office building. She took the elevator to the top floor where Matthew's secretary greeted her. She was an attractive woman in her thirties and immaculately dressed in a narrow, navy-blue skirt, heels and suit jacket, and sporting a startlingly tall bouffant hairdo.

She ushered Kate into a room with a long table in the center and twenty chairs surrounding it. The large windows offered a spectacular view of the city. The secretary offered beverages and Kate chose hot herb tea with lemon, which arrived to her in fine china. She was advised that the team would be joining her shortly as soon as they returned from looking at a new property.

Kate sipped her tea and then made a second cup with the extra hot water provided. Then, the door opened and Matthew greeted her warmly, followed by no less than ten other men in business suits. She was introduced to each in turn and forgot all their names immediately. Everyone sat down and several opened ledgers and notebooks while pulling fountain pens out of their shirt pocket protectors. Matthew sat across the table from Kate and began.

"Kate, we have all spent time reviewing your excellently-prepared proposal. It is clear you have done your homework and that you have a keen idea of this undertaking's potential. We also realize that there are many players involved in this inherited property. Your mother, your Uncle Allen, and your Aunt Dorothy are, of course, the primary beneficiaries. But clearly, you have taken the lead on behalf of your side of our family to carry through with this business opportunity.

"Last month, we sent our international attorney and a mining expert from Detroit down to Honduras to do some additional investigating. Their findings substantiated your research and enhanced our understanding of practices in that country. We are interested in offering the family a set fee for the mining lease on the properties. In addition, there will be royalties paid on a quarterly basis for the actual value of the gold, silver, and copper extracted. I expect the family will be pleased with our generous offer."

Matthew pushed a single sheet of paper across the table to her. Kate looked down and almost burst into tears. She was too excited and nervous to read it fully, but she clearly saw a figure for more than one million dollars. She stared at the number, waiting for the decimal to shift and reveal something in her realm of understanding. The decimal point stayed put.

She looked up at Matthew and then slowly made eye contact with each man at the table. Finally, holding her hands together under the table so they did not shake, she said that she would be happy to present this offer to the family.

"Well, of course," Matthew said, "you should share this information right away, but we will send the offer in writing to each of them for their review. We will advise they each seek their own legal counsel to ensure protection of their interests and to make sure they understand what they are signing. Our desire would be to wrap up the legal paperwork by August so we can begin working the mines by the first of next year."

Kate smiled broadly and said, "That would be magnificent."

They all shook hands. Matthew walked her to the elevator where she became so lost in daydreaming she almost forgot to get off when the doors opened on the first floor. The chauffeur drove Kate back to Maggie and Jeffrey. As soon as Kate walked in the door, she burst into tears. She could hardly control her voice enough to explain to her sister what had happened. Maggie asked the maid to fetch a bottle of champagne and the two drank a toast to the good fortune of their family.

Everyone was so excited that the family spent a small fortune on long distance calls to each other. They were all immensely grateful to Kate for carrying it all through. She dismissed their praise, insisting it was her father who had kept it alive... plus Maggie had made it possible by marrying an amazing business tycoon.

THE SIGNING COMMENCED IN mid-July. By mid-August, Ginger, Allen, and Dottie received the first disbursements for the lease. Ginger immediately divided her share in thirds for herself, Kate, and Maggie. Maggie opened a bank account in her name, for the first time, and declared she would save the money for Jeffrey.

Though Kate had fond memories of their time at the beach cottage, she understood it was an especially unsafe location in the event of a hurricane. They had a near miss the year before when a hurricane required them to go inland and spend the night on cots in a high school gym. When they returned home, the place was a sandy swamp. They dragged the mattresses and sofa out into the sun and left them for days before they fully dried. Luckily, these were the only overly absorbent items. The clothes, bedding, and curtains were fine after a marathon day at the laundromat.

This incident had left Kate feeling she and her girls were too exposed and vulnerable at the cottage. She used her share of the disbursement to move them to a brick house a half a mile inland on a quiet, unimproved road. The back yard was adjacent to an orange grove and had a fig tree and a coconut palm. The artist who built the house had incorporated broken tiles into elaborate mosaics on the windowsills, fireplace hearth, and front step. There were neighbors close enough to hail in an emergency, but not close enough to know their business.

Kate continued working at the Fish Hatchery. She enrolled Eliza in kindergarten the next fall, helped Victoria with her reading skills, and kept her car well maintained. After visiting several second-hand stores, she bought a typewriter at a pawnshop, and enrolled in a correspondence course in creative writing. She worked on her assignments late into the evening and received excellent grades.

Ladies Home Journal published her first short story the following year, then *Reader's Digest* published another. When she received a second disbursement from her mother, she asked her boss if it would be possible for her to become a part-time employee so she had more time to write. She was working on a novel and it was coming along well. She thought it would be publishable when finished. Her employer said no—not out of lack of compassion—but because government jobs just were not that flexible. She continued, waiting for the right time to launch her new career.

Meanwhile, Ginger sold the Dairy Queen. It never really kept her interest and she wanted to do something more befitting her character. She used the proceeds from the sale to lease a storefront and opened "Granny's Yarn." She stocked a beautiful array of yarns in bins lining one wall, as well as quilting fabrics in colorful prints, crochet supplies, needlepoint kits, sewing supplies, and Ray's miniature dollhouse furniture. She taught classes right in the middle of the store and—even when no classes were in session—she welcomed like-minded women to sit and do handwork in an odd assortment of refurbished rocking chairs.

There, they would spend afternoons "spinning yarns," thereby completing the *entendre* of the business name. Her cleaning skills had not improved over the years and she hired a young woman to come in twice a week to tidy up and clean the store. Kate thought she should also have the cleaning lady come to Ginger's house occasionally, but Ginger thought that was completely unnecessary.

The following year, Ginger, and by extension Kate, began receiving mining extraction royalties. They were substantial. Kate resigned from her clerical job, made arrangements with the bank for a twenty-year mortgage to purchase the house she had been renting, and began writing full-time.

Much to her surprise and pleasure, she received a couple of letters each year from Bret. They were rich and colorful in details about his life and she happily reciprocated. He was interested in purebred Arabians and had started working with a few horses on his parent's farm in rural Oklahoma. He found the horses at auctions and picked them up inexpensively in a place where quarter horses were what ranchers wanted. Kate loved that he had gravitated to horses and she never failed to comment on his progress, sharing her own tricks she had developed in her younger years.

Their friendship lasted throughout the years, even after Bret was married with his own children, then divorced, then married again. Though they never met again face to face, their affection transcended both time and space late into their lives.

As for Kate, she was thrilled to live vicariously through the loves of her children's lives and pained to suffer with them through breakups, divorces, and heartaches. The girls did reconnect with their father in their late twenties and established a lifelong bond with him. Over the years, Kate softened her views on homosexuality and grew to understand it was in the shadows all around her.

She remembered her first marriage fondly up until she was hurt by Thomas' infidelity. Kate eventually came to the conclusion that having a best friend as a husband was not the worst fate one could suffer. He had been fun, funny, caring, and lacking that veiled threat of testosterone poisoning. In the 1990s, when she was in her seventies, her favorite television show was *Will & Grace*. It helped normalize that which had once seemed extraordinary and softened her heart toward her first husband.

Creating stories fueled her life and became a balm to her soul. She connected with many readers through her craft and enjoyed communicating with her fans through the mail. She especially worked hard to channel her grandmother Mimi in attitude about her own life and in wisdom when it came to advising her children. Even though she was not fond of wearing hats, on days when she needed a little extra comfort, she would don a wide-brimmed straw sun hat and think of her.

Honor

I N MAY 1996, KATE received a call from Maggie saying Ginger had died in her sleep in Vero Beach. At eighty-seven, her passing was not completely unexpected, but she had not been ill. The death certificate said she died of heart failure, meaning the examining doctor did not know the cause. Obviously, her heart had stopped, so it was an easy answer to write on the form.

Kate had relocated to South Carolina many years earlier and, sadly, had not seen or spoken to her mother for more than twenty years. She agreed to meet Maggie in Vero Beach in August to help settle their mother's estate, which was without a will to provide guidance. Their first order of business was to relocate Ray into an assisted living facility. He had been Ginger's companion for nearly forty years. Kate and Maggie agreed that part of her estate funds would go to his care.

They planned to sell the house, but first needed to clean it out. They spent three weeks going through the vast accumulation of a lifetime. Together, they discovered photos they had never seen of Parke and Ginger in their younger years. A studio portrait of a devastatingly handsome young Parke, as well as a snapshot of him in his cavalry attire lounging in a tavern in France, would be scanned and reproduced so they could each have a copy. Photos of Ginger in a variety of poses were divided between them. They also found images of themselves, long forgotten, including one of Kate as a girl astride the towering Standardbred at the country club and her Sweet Sixteen studio portrait.

Each evening they returned to the Driftwood where they shared a room. They talked late into the night catching up. Jeffrey had died in his late thirties, but Kate never knew the details of his ordeal until now. After losing Matthew to cancer, Maggie had exhausted nearly everything she had saved and that Matthew had left her to care for Jeffrey. His hospital bills were exorbitant and she spared nothing for him to receive the very best care. After Jeffrey's death, she returned to Florida often to visit Ginger. They had always remained close.

Beyond the photos, there was a lot of normal debris to sort and dispose of: utility bills, letters from friends and relatives, and mementos of bygone days. As they sorted, they discussed items each would like to keep. Both were agreeable and no disagreements ensued. Kate would be taking Parke's golf trophies, his cavalry boots, the small table that Baba made rise on that mysterious day so long ago, her mother's large wooden kitchen cutting board, and the watercolor painting of the castle in the clouds that her parents always giggled about. The majority of the furniture went to an auction house; everyday kitchenware and clothing went to charities.

When the house was cleared out and they were ready to list it for sale with an agent, they went to the funeral home to collect

Ginger's ashes. Maggie told Kate that Ginger said many times over the years that she wished to be buried with Parke. The sisters went to the cemetery to visit his grave, then spoke with the manager of the property. The plots next to Parke's grave had been sold and occupied by the newly deceased. He was unable to honor their request to put Ginger next to Parke.

They left the cemetery to have dinner and over several glasses of wine, they made a plan. On their final evening in Vero Beach, they sat in Kate's car on the stretch of road beside the cemetery. From this vantage point they could see the manager's house. They watched him walk down to close and lock the gate at dusk. They waited another hour for his front window lights to go off.

Kate had purchased a shovel and two folding ladders at the hardware store. Dressed entirely in black with hats pulled down low on their brows, the sisters pulled their tools out of the trunk and slipped down along the fence adjacent to the woods. Hearts pounding, Kate propped one ladder along the fence and climbed to the top. Maggie handed her the other ladder for Kate to reach down and prop on the other side. They both climbed over, realized they forgot the shovel and Ginger's box of ashes on the other side. Kate, in whispers, made Maggie go back over for them.

The moon provided enough light to navigate between the headstones to their father's grave, but they lit a match briefly to make sure they had the right grave. They took turns with the shovel removing the sod, then digging a hole about two feet deep. They laid the box of ashes carefully in the bottom, took a moment to silently say their individual goodbyes, then covered the hole. Before packing the sod back down on top, Maggie took flower bulbs from her pocket and poked them down into the soft, freshly-turned soil. They then silently returned to the ladders, climbed over the fence, and packed the evidence of their caper back into the trunk. They drove down around the corner before Kate turned the headlights on. After taking a few deep breaths, they started laughing uncontrollably.

Honoring their mother's wish felt like the best tribute they could give her. They would both be sore in the morning from climbing the ladder and digging with the shovel at their ages.

"We could have been arrested as grave robbers," mused Maggie.

"But we didn't take anything. The charges wouldn't stick," Kate told her.

"What about breaking and entering?"

"We didn't break anything either," reasoned Kate.

"Trespassing?" tried Maggie.

"Okay, that might cost us a fine. But no jail time for first offenders."

"Oh, you don't know my life. What makes you think I don't have a record?" Maggie quipped deadpan. And they both laughed.

They talked about how Parke would have loved what they did. He would want Ginger to be with him and he did not like to see her disappointed.

It was with sincere affection that they parted ways at the airport for Maggie to fly home. Kate drove back to South Carolina with the treasures gleaned from her parent's house, thinking of her sister. They had shared their most formative years growing up in Pleasant Valley. Despite everything, they were witness to each other's lives in a way that was irreplaceable. Kate truly felt sorry for what her sister had endured and wished she could go back in time and be there for her.

It was only then that Kate finally let go of her harbored jealousy and resentment. As she made her way home, she let those petty feelings fly away for good into a beautiful orange and pink sunset sky. She knew Mimi would be pleased.

Notes From the Author

Although this is a work of fiction, it is deeply intertwined with my family history. In the late-1980s, my mother, Nancy Lusk Purcell, then in her late sixties, set out to earn her Bachelor's degree from the University of Oklahoma. As part of her liberal arts coursework, she started writing a book. The first half of *Beneath a Barren Sky* draws from those writings, as well as stories she told me over the years. In 2002, my mother died leaving the story hanging.

As I worked on this, it occurred to me often that the characters would be recognizable to living relatives. My mother's family has always been widely dispersed and many of them I either never knew or only met briefly. Therefore, I have relied on my mother's spoken memories, fictional creative writing, and my desire to create a story that hangs together for the reader.

About Author

Carolyn Purcell Jaco grew up in rural Maine with four sisters. She studied literature at Montana State University and earned an MLS degree from the University of Oklahoma, focusing on history and cultural geography with an award-winning thesis. Through four decades, Carolyn's career in museums included positions at the Museum of the Rockies in Bozeman, Montana, and the Columbia Gorge Discovery Center in The Dalles, Oregon. Now retired in rural Oklahoma, she is a fulltime fiction writer.

Also by this author: *The Nature of Wayfinding*, 2023, Scissortail Press.

Please review this book on Amazon. Reach the author at calyjaco@gmail.com, on Facebook, and on LinkedIn.

www.ingramcontent.com/pod-product-compliance
Lightning Source LLC
Chambersburg PA
CBHW060633260626
47161CB00008B/2880